IN AMERICA, Damien Thorn is about to begin his unstoppable climb to power, a climb that will only end when all of mankind lies beneath his evil sway . . .

IN ENGLAND, the American ambassador, hounded by terrifying nightmare visions, is about to commit suicide in a particularly gruesome way . . .

IN EGYPT, the Aswan Dam is about to burst, causing unthinkable death and devastation, and bringing the Middle East one critical step closer to war . . .

IN AUSTRALIA, terrible drought is threatening to bring an entire nation crumbling down . . .

AND SOMEWHERE, a child is about to be born, humanity's long-awaited last hope for salvation from the all-consuming flames of hell . . .

THE FINAL CONFLICT

Great Movies Available in SIGNET Editions

- [ ] THE OMEN by David Seltzer. (#J8180—$1.95)
- [ ] DAMIEN—OMEN II by Joseph Howard. (#J8164—$1.95)*
- [ ] THE STUD by Jackie Collins. (#J9187—$1.95)†
- [ ] INSIDE MOVES by Todd Walton. (#E9661—$2.50)
- [ ] COMA by Robin Cook. (#E9756—$2.75)
- [ ] PENTIMENTO (including "Julia") by Lillian Hellman. (#E9797—$2.75)
- [ ] KRAMER VS. KRAMER by Avery Corman. (#E8914—$2.50)
- [ ] SEMI-TOUGH by Dan Jenkins. (#J8184—$1.95)
- [ ] I NEVER PROMISED YOU A ROSE GARDEN by Joanne Greenberg. (#E9700—$2.25)
- [ ] ONE FLEW OVER THE CUCKOO'S NEST by Ken Kesey. (#E8867—$2.25)
- [ ] GOOD GUYS WEAR BLACK by Max Franklin. (#E7972—$1.75)
- [ ] NORTH DALLAS FORTY by Peter Gent. (#E8906—$2.50)
- [ ] THE SWARM by Arthur Herzog. (#E8079—$2.25)
- [ ] THE SERIAL by Cyra McFadden. (#E9267—$2.50)

* Price slightly higher in Canada
† Not available in Canada

THE FINAL CONFLICT

a novel by

Gordon McGill

from the screenplay by

Andrew Birkin

A SIGNET BOOK

NEW AMERICAN LIBRARY

TIMES MIRROR

Copyright © 1980 by Twentieth Century-Fox
Film Corporation

Ø

SIGNET, SIGNET CLASSICS, MENTOR, PLUME, MERIDIAN AND NAL
BOOKS are published by The New American Library, Inc.,
1633 Broadway, New York, New York 10019.

First Printing, December, 1980

1 2 3 4 5 6 7 8 9

—Thou hast conquered, O pale Galilean;
  The world has grown grey from thy breath;
  We have drunken of things Lethean,
  And fed on the fullness of death.
  Laurel is green for a season,
  And love is sweet for a day;
  But love grows bitter with treason,
  And laurel outlives not May.

                    —Swinburne,
                      "Hymn to Proserpine"

Preface

The astronomer was not a religious man. When he gazed through his telescope, he saw the sky and not the heavens. As a youth he had believed in the God of his parents, but when he was a man, he put away childish things. To John Favell, the secrets of the universe were directly related to the wonders of mathematics and physics. The sight through the two-hundred-inch telescope at the Fernbank Observatory on the Sussex Downs was fascinating enough in itself without bringing in some Supreme Being to complicate matters.

That night there was a minimum of cloud cover and the routine work had been completed early. Now he was free to indulge himself in surveying the skies, taking photographic scans, each night adding another set of prints to his library, building up a cosmic atlas.

He sipped his coffee and glanced up to see if everything was ready. The observatory, dominated by the massive telescope, was silent. His technician sat beside it, hands on the controls, looking back at him, waiting expectantly, like a dog about to go for a walk.

Favell leaned across his desk and squinted into a television monitor.

"Where are we going tonight?" he muttered.

"Cassiopeia, sir," said the technician.

Briefly the astronomer's mind was clouded by a fragment of memory, something he could not place, but it passed as quickly as it had come, and he settled himself in front of the screen.

"Cassiopeia," he repeated. "Right ascension. One hour sixteen minutes twelve; select declination at twenty-two degrees on an eight-by-four ratio."

He grunted in satisfaction as the telescope picked out the area in question. Again he issued his instructions, as he had done almost each night for the past five years, scanning the skies and making his notes. When he saw what he wanted, he sat back.

"Hold. Okay, hard copy."

He pushed himself away from his desk, moved across the room, and waited until the scan of the starfield slid from a chute by the side of the telescope. He picked it up carefully, took it to a light box, spread it on the glass, and gazed at it.

He narrowed his eyes and sniffed.

"Odd," he said. A single syllable, a merest whisper, but enough to make the technician turn in his seat and look questioningly at him.

"We took a similar scan the other day, didn't we?"

The technician nodded. "Monday, sir."

He reached into a filing cabinet, selected a transparency, and handed it over. Favell slipped the second scan under the first and blinked.

"There has been movement," he said in a flat voice. "Three suns."

And now it was the technician's turn to frown.

Favell looked up, his face flushed. "Get the historical records of this field. Go right back."

He watched his assistant hunt among the filing cabinets, then walked to the telescope, gazed out to the stars, and pursed his lips. Mathematics and physics, the only certainties, he thought. It was all so obvious, yet everyone else, at parties and dinners, would ask him about silly things; UFOs, little green men. It was the mystery and the nonsense that excited them, and sometimes it was difficult to hide the disdain he felt for them.

The technician tapped his arm and handed him a pile of transparencies. He studied them and turned back to the young man.

"What would you say?" he asked.

The technician shrugged and smiled, almost apologetically. "I'd say I was dreaming."

"Quite." He gestured toward the monitor. "What is the rate of acceleration?"

The young man checked the monitor. "A couple of thousand parsecs minimum." He looked back. "Seems like we're in for one hell of a bang."

Favell shook his head in irritation. "An alignment, not a collision." The curiosity was building in him now, and he drummed his fingers impatiently. "Transfer to the simulator," he said. "Let's see if we can get an accurate schedule prediction."

The technician snapped a button on the monitor, and the two men stared at the screen, watching the projected flight paths of the three suns. Their eyes flicked back and forth between the converging dots and the digital readout in the corner of the screen.

As he watched the figures spin, Favell recalled the flash of memory of a few moments earlier.

Cassiopeia. The priest had mentioned Cassiopeia. Three years ago at the international convention in Nice, the Italian priest in the cassock who gate-crashed one of the meetings; he had asked the delegates to watch out for three stars coming together in the region of Cassiopeia. He had implored them to keep a watch and to let him know.

He remembered the scene clearly; the priest was so tense, yet so dignified, and the delegates permitted him to speak. No one had mocked the man, for they respected his sincerity. It was only when he had gone that they laughed among themselves.

"Sir." The technician was pointing at the screen.

The dots converged, pulsated rapidly, and emitted a series of expanding rings. The digital readout had stopped, the figures standing out starkly against the background:

002. 26. 00. 24. 03. 82.

It was a time and a date. The voice of the priest echoed in his brain; insane words about the rebirth of the Messiah, the return of the Christ Child.

24. 03. 82.

It was a date of birth.

Instinctively and precisely, John Favell made the sign of the cross.

PART
ONE

1

For two hours the massive drill had worked cease-lessly, chewing its way through the clay ten feet be-low the streets of Chicago, gouging a tunnel at the rate of one meter every six minutes, sucking the sweating clay through its snout and excreting the de-bris onto a conveyor belt at its rear.

Behind the drill head, a small man worked silently, sifting the debris on the belt and occasionally playing a cooling hose over the rotating blades. The air was foul in the tunnel, and Joey dripped with sweat. It was the worst job in the world, he would say to his friends, but he took a perverse pride in it. Once, after a few beers, he had compared it to a preview of Hell.

Joey sensed trouble a second before it happened. The drill seemed to pause, a hiccup in the flow, then it bucked upward. The throb changed to a screech, and Joey ducked as chunks of brick and concrete were spat back at him through the body of the machine and into the wall of the tunnel.

Cursing, he yelled for the operator to hit the switch. When the power was cut, he jumped forward, edging around the drill and searching for damage. Wedging himself against the tunnel, he looked down and cursed again; a brick wall. The drill was meant for clay, not brick. If there was any damage, there would be delay, and delay meant lost pay. Venomously he swore at the faceless surveyors and architects, men he despised, men in suits who never did their homework and left the men at the sharp end to run into trouble.

A moment later there were others around him and the supervisor was climbing next to him, staring at the pieces of brickwork dislodged by the drill.

Sulking, Joey stood back and waited. It was nothing, the boss was saying; just a basement wall, the remains of the old Thorn Museum. Joey remembered the place. It had burned down years ago; fifteen, maybe twenty years. He remembered the story in the papers; a mystery fire, no one ever charged.

He spat into the clay and swore again at the surveyors. If they knew about the wall, why did they send in the drill with the soft head? He continued swearing and spitting until the boss turned and told him to be quiet.

And then he was alone again. They were going to blast through and hope for the best.

The machine coughed into life again, but this time Joey kept well back. He reached for the cooling hose, but dropped it as he saw something glinting inside one of the lumps of clay. Reaching out with both hands, he wrestled the lump off the conveyor belt, turned it onto its side, and dropped it onto the tunnel floor, where it broke up. Joey bent forward, then stepped back, shuddering slightly. Protruding from the clay were charred bones and a piece of skull. Scattered among the bones lay dull metallic sticks.

Gingerly he picked up the nearest, rubbing the clay with callused fingers. It was a knife, with a long blade and an ornate handle. More than just a knife, he thought; an old-fashioned weapon, a dagger. He ran his thumb down the blade and grunted. It was still sharp. He scraped at the hilt and saw in the gloom that it had been worked in the shape of a crucifix, the figure of Christ spread round it, the clay etched into the broken body and the agonized face.

He glanced back along the tunnel. No one could see him. Joey was a smart little man. He added up two and two and made four. Daggers and bones meant a murder. Someone had died a terrible death in that fire, but if he was to report it, the daggers would have to be handed in to the authorities.

He had forgotten about the drill. All he wanted was to collect the daggers; one, two, three, scrabbling in the dirt, throwing away the bones, piling the daggers under the conveyor belt until he could smuggle them out.

The pawnbroker gazed at the daggers and sniffed.

"Probably some spic gang," he said.

Joey slapped his forehead with the palm of his hand. "C'mon," he pleaded. "Can't you see they're old?"

The pawnbroker shrugged.

"Must be old," he persisted. "Must be worth a fortune."

"Is that so?"

Eventually Joey gave in. From long experience he

knew that arguing with pawnbrokers was a waste of time. It always came down to the old line—take it or leave it. Joey took the handful of grubby bills and left the shop.

He slouched into the rain, counting the money. It wasn't much but it was better than nothing. Buried treasure was something that came with the job—the occasional coin, bits of jewelry dropped down a sewer, all tax-free. But he should have received more for the daggers. On the other hand, it was an unexpected bonus, a windfall, a godsend. He pushed the bar door open; Clancy's Bar and Grill. Joey was superstitious. You don't keep this kind of money. It should go on a horse or a bottle.

He hoisted himself onto a stool and ordered a shot of Scotch and a Michelob chaser. Another and he was buying for the barman; another and he was buying for his friends.

In the morning he was too sick to go to work and lost a day's pay.

The daggers lay unnoticed and unclaimed for a month before one of the scouts from the uptown auctioneers saw them in the rear of the window and bought them. Two days later they were on show in the auction room as Lot 7, laid out on velvet in a neat row. The seven faces of Christ gleamed now, and the blades were so finely polished that they reflected the light of the room.

The auction itself was uninspired. It was the slow season, with few bidders, and only one man seemed interested in Lot 7. He stood at the back of the hall and needed to bid only twice before making the purchase.

As he drove back to his apartment, the man glanced

at the daggers wrapped in cloth lying on the passenger seat. He was curious about them. Something nagged at his brain, and he tried without success to dredge up some memory, something he had read years ago.

When he reached his apartment he went straight to his study and laid the daggers on his desk. For a moment he gazed at them, then picked up the nearest, testing the weight and the balance. Gently he ran the blade across his palm and yelped as it sliced through a layer of skin, drawing a trickle of blood. He wrapped a handkerchief around his hand and held the dagger by thumb and forefinger, his thumb covering the face of Christ. Slowly he raised the dagger six inches above his desk diary and dropped it. The blade cut through the book and imbedded itself in the desk.

Christ on the cross shuddered and swayed until the man pulled the dagger out and inspected the damage. It was a vicious weapon, the blade triangular so that any wound inflicted would take a long time to heal. He shivered and moved to the shelves, selected three books, and returned to the desk. Settling himself, he began to read, caressing the hilt of the dagger as he turned the pages.

An hour later he reached for the phone, tapped out a number, and waited.

"Father Doolan, please," he said when the number answered, and he was not surprised to find his voice hoarse with excitement.

At first the passengers nearest to the young priest on the Alitalia Boeing 747 were glad of his company. Those nervous of flying took some comfort in his silent prayers as the great aircraft shuddered up the runway at Kennedy Airport, New York, and heaved

11

itself into the clear sky, banking east over Long Island.

But as the flight progressed, they began to feel a little concerned. Why was he so fidgety? Did he know something they did not? And what was so important about the package on his lap that he clutched onto it all the time, not letting go even when the meal was brought round? By the end of the flight, as they landed in Rome, they were glad to be safely on the ground.

At the customs desk, the officer apologized to the priest for asking him to open his bags. The man was embarrassed, challenging the integrity of a man of the cloth, but he had little choice. These days the drug smugglers knew all the tricks and were quite capable of passing themselves off as churchmen.

He blinked when he opened the package and saw the daggers, but even before he had time to ask about them, the priest had flipped a bill of sale in front of him, stamped by a Chicago auctioneer.

As he waved the priest through, the customs officer gazed after him, wondering what on earth an American cleric was doing in Rome with a handful of daggers. God moves in mysterious ways, he thought, then turned to the next passenger and forgot all about Father Doolan.

The priest hired a car at the airport and drove south through the night. As he neared his destination, he checked his map and looked at his watch. Soon it would be dawn. He yawned, stretched, and eased the little Fiat through the country lanes past sleeping farms and villages toward Subiaco.

It was still dark when he stopped the car and turned off the engine. The unaccustomed silence made him shiver. He got out and gazed up at the monastery, a crumbling black relic rising out of the hilltop, the ragged roof jagged against the night sky.

As he climbed toward it, he was conscious of the age of the place, aware for the first time of a sense of history. He could imagine the centuries of turmoil, the constant battle between good and evil fought on this soil since the fortress had been built in the days of Herod. He felt small and insignificant; he stopped and gazed at the ancient door now only a few yards away and could imagine the monks worshiping here for centuries. He shivered. Never had he felt such awe, such a sense of continuity, never in the eastern cities of America.

He pushed the heavy door, and it creaked open. Slowly he made his way into the monastery and tapped lightly on an inner door. In turn the smaller door opened, and at first Father Doolan could see nothing. The shape was tall and black and beckoning him in, and, as Doolan looked up, he was startled to discover that the monk was black, as black as a Harlem night, and tall, with a goatee beard. The monk turned and gestured for him to follow him down a series of flagstones and into a small crypt.

Clutching the daggers, he gazed around the tiny room. He was alone. The black priest had gone.

The crypt was dominated by a cross, and Doolan could make out in the gloom a small tabernacle set into the far wall. As he knelt at the foot of the cross, he was aware that someone had entered the crypt. He turned to see a priest behind him, a stocky man with a broad forehead and an aquiline nose, a man in his fifties.

"Father De Carlo?" Doolan whispered.

The priest nodded and told him to rise. Doolan

13

stood up and handed over the daggers, waiting, hoping for some sort of explanation, but the black monk had returned and was beckoning to him again. Maybe he would be told later, but now, all he wanted was to sleep.

Father De Carlo waited until he was alone, then took the daggers from the package and gazed at each one before laying them on the altar before the cross. He knelt in prayer, thanking his God for their return; the ancient daggers of Megiddo, from the town once known as Armageddon.

He rose, picked them up, held them to the cross, then reached into his cassock for a leather pouch and placed them inside. That done, he moved to the tabernacle, opened the doors, kissed the pouch, and laid it in the center.

Silently he gave a prayer of thanks; for the Englishman John Favell, the stargazer who had discovered the time of the rebirth and who had sent word to Subiaco; for the return of the daggers, the only weapons which could put an end to the life of the Anti-Christ.

Twice before the attempt had been made, each time ending in failure and tragedy, but this time there could be no failure, for the Christ Child was coming. The Anti-Christ still lived.

The Final Conflict was about to begin.

2

In a small screening room high above the Chicago streets, the blinds had been drawn and in the semi-darkness a group of men waited nervously. One smoked incessantly, another moved around the room touching the backs of the chairs. A third bit his fingernails. They talked loudly to one another in short disjointed sentences, and they laughed a lot. Their anticipation and apprehension could almost be smelled.

The door opened and a beam of light from the corridor zipped into the room. For a moment, Damien Thorn stood framed in the doorway. The chairman of the board, six feet tall, slim, dark, and handsome, he had recently been described by an influential magazine as one of the three most eligible bachelors in the Western world. As majority stockholder in the Thorn Corporation, he was certainly one of the richest men in the world, and he had not yet reached his thirty-third birthday. He moved into the room followed by his personal assistant.

"Gentlemen," said Damien.

"Damien," they chorused, dodging around as he glided between them and took his seat in the front row.

"You all know Harvey Dean."

Dean nodded a greeting at each of them. A slightly built, dapper man, forty years old, he exuded a nervous energy. His eyes darted from one man to the next as he ushered Damien to his seat. Each man smiled back at him, for Harvey Dean was the access route to the chairman. One executive had commented that Dean was to Damien what Bormann was to Hitler and what Haldeman was to Nixon. The man had been fired within the hour.

The two men settled themselves, waited until the others were seated, and then Damien snapped his fingers and the lights went out. The others blinked, but the eyes of Damien Thorn, the man born of a jackal, quickly adjusted to the dark.

A moment later the screen exploded into light. A blizzard raged before them, slowly dying out, the screen showing an empty desert landscape.

The men sitting behind Damien held their breaths as the voice of the narrator boomed out from four speakers.

"Fifty thousand years ago, mankind faced its first major threat of extinction. . . ."

Damien scratched his ear.

"A devastation wrought by Nature. The Ice Age. It lasted five thousand years, rendered four-fifths of the earth's surface uninhabitable, and wiped out all but the hardiest of nature's creations."

The screen showed a cave and primitive drawings.

16

"One of those few was Man," intoned the narrator. "From that devastation dawned a new age—and a new hope. Phoenixlike, man arose from the frozen wilderness, and set forth upon his dream."

Now the scene was an arid plantation, destroyed by drought.

"Mankind has endured many catastrophes since then, but none so grave as the one which faces him today. The economic crisis of the past decade has brought inflation, famine, and chaos to every corner of the globe."

Almost unnoticed, Damien licked his bottom lip. One of the men behind him nudged his neighbor and winked.

"Some label it the Great Recession," continued the narration. "Others are calling it Armageddon—that final upheaval of the world foretold by the prophets of old. But amid all the pessimism, one voice rings out its faith in the future. The voice of Thorn. . . ."

All in the group, as one, leaned deeper in their seats as the Thorn Building came up on the screen, the building in which they were sitting, a glittering skyscraper rearing into the night sky, its lighted windows forming a giant T.

"Wherever famine or disease has struck, the Thorn Corporation has been first in the field. . . ."

And by way of illustration, a map of the world flashed onto the screen, lit up with a myriad of bulbs, each one pinpointing a Thorn operation.

". . . waging a relentless war on want by channeling its resources, technology, and research into projects that not only aid and relieve the suffering, but lay the foundation of the future prosperity for all."

There was a slight pause before the voice of a second narrator took over:

"Thorn . . . the world's leading light in building a new tomorrow."

The commercial ended. The house lights came up once more and each member of the group tried not to blink or show any sign of strain. They gazed, all of them, at the back of Damien's head. Eventually, after a few moments' silence, one of them cleared his throat.

"Well?" An apprehensive gulp.

"I make that four mixed metaphors, two split infinitives, and a floating gerundive," said Damien quietly.

Everyone laughed except Dean.

"I don't think viewers pay too much attention to that kind of stuff," the advertising man said.

Damien turned and stood up, looking at them for the first time.

"No, you're right," he said, "and they won't pay much attention to that kind of sanctimonious bullshit either."

He allowed the word to hang rotting in the air as his employees shifted in their seats.

"I said I wanted action, not words. I want to *see* Thorn at work, not hear about it."

Chins dropped onto chests and the men blinked, trying to duck away from Damien's gaze.

"A thousand starving kids clamoring for a bellyful of Thorn soya," he continued. "Thorn medical teams at work. Thorn construction. Thorn engineering." He paused and turned his attention to the man who had first broken the silence.

"Instead of which you spend half of the commercial giving us a third-grade potted history of the Ice Age."

The barb went deep, and the man quietly wriggled inside his five-hundred-dollar suit. All that time, he

18

thought, all that money and creative effort, for what? To feel like a gaffed fish.

Damien had turned to his assistant now, ignoring the others.

"Do we have any footage of the Australian Drought Relief?"

Dean nodded an affirmative. "But it's nothing special," he said. "Most of it has been seen on TV already."

He turned back to the advertising men. "All right, we'll find something for you. In the meantime, go on screening the old commercial. I don't want to see that one"—he gestured toward the blank screen—"go out."

With that he sliced through them again, Dean at his heels.

"Goodbye, Mr. Thorn," they mumbled, as one, but this time there was no reply.

Damien moved smartly along a corridor toward his office.

"What have we got coming up?" he asked as Dean caught up with him.

"Botswana next week, then the Aswan Dam at the end of the month."

Dean nodded to himself. Botswana had been a problem, but the team which had been infiltrated into the country had forecast that the coup would take place within three or four days. There would be havoc. There would be thousands of refugee mouths to feed. As for the dam, preparations were still being made, but the operation had every chance of success. They had the best explosives men in the business. Paul Buher, president of the corporation, was handling the project, and Buher had rarely been known to fail.

As they reached the reception area to his suite of

offices, two women glanced up at Damien, but he ignored them and swept through.

"Could we get a film unit down to Botswana in time?"

"Sure," said Dean. "But we can't put our relief teams in till after the coup, and no one's sure how long that will take."

Dean followed his boss into the office and closed the door behind them, thinking back to his first glimpse of the suite of rooms. Like every other newcomer he had expected chrome and steel, glass and leather, something overtly masculine, and had been shocked at first by the paneled walls, the Regency chairs, the ornately carved desk, the hunting prints. The place was a throwback to more leisurely days.

Paul Buher had once raised laughter by suggesting that he would have been more comfortable in a powdered wig and breeches. Only Buher had the confidence to make such remarks, and even he, number two in the corporation, would not make such a comment lightly. He would first judge Damien's mood, and he would say it to his face, never behind his back. Nor would he implement any decisions without Damien's approval. He had learned that rule from Richard Thorn, twenty years ago, when he had become president.

Damien moved past his desk and gazed out over the rooftops of Chicago.

"Okay, then, it will have to be the dam. Can you arrange for a unit to be out there when it goes?"

Dean nodded.

"And make sure they give our relief teams plenty of coverage. Don't let the Red Cross beat them to it."

Dean smiled at the idea and came up with one of his own.

"Why don't you go?" he suggested. "That would be a coup. Damien Thorn supervising the relief work in person."

Damien turned and shook his head, smiling to himself.

"I have to stay here," he said.

"What for?" Dean searched his mind for a reason and could think of none. There was nothing to stay for.

"To be on hand when the President calls for me."

From anyone else, the statement would have sounded absurd, pretentious. Maybe it was some kind of joke, but Damien Thorn did not make jokes.

"He's going to offer me the post of Ambassador to Great Britain."

Dean blinked, shrugged his shoulders, lost for words, and watched as Damien moved to the bookshelves which lined one of the walls.

"Are you familiar with the Book of Hebron?"

"The book of who?" First Great Britain, he thought, now Hebron. The man was talking in riddles.

Damien took a book from the shelf.

"The Book of Hebron, one of the obscure books of the Apocrypha."

Dean shrugged again, waiting and hoping for enlightenment. Damien opened the book and selected a passage.

" 'And it shall come to pass,' " he read, " 'that in the end days the Beast shall reign one hundred score and thirty days and nights, and the faithful shall cry unto the Lord: "wherefore are Thou in the day of evil?" ' "

" 'And the Lord shall hear their prayers, and out of the angel isle he shall bring forth a deliverer, the holy

Lamb of God, who shall do battle with the Beast ...
and shall utterly destroy him.' "

He closed the book and clasped it in front of him.

"That the Beast shall reign one hundred score and
thirty days and nights is a rather fancy way of saying
seven years, the length of time I've been head of
Thorn Corporation.

" 'And out of the angel isle the Lord shall bring
forth a deliverer.' "

He paused. "The angel isle. The original Latin has
ex insula Angelorum." He shrugged. "England."

Dean frowned, trying to piece together the puzzle
and slowly a possibility came to him; reluctantly and
painfully.

"Only it won't be the Beast who is utterly
destroyed," said Damien. "It will be the Nazarene."

It was too much too quick. Dean could scarcely
take it in. His mind rejected it and turned, as a defense mechanism, to practicalities.

"But what about our ambassador? The man who's
in office in London?"

Damien merely smiled. It was the only reply Dean
was to get. For the moment.

3
_____

The chase seemed to have lasted forever, and he was exhausted. He had no breath. His legs were heavy, and when he tried to cough, he retched. There was no moisture in him. He was kicking up the dust of the desert, and he could see the trees ahead, their branches waving at him in the breeze as if in encouragement, urging him forward to safety; but he knew that he would never reach the trees. He had known from the beginning. He had always known, yet still he kept running, his feet no longer rising from the ground. It was as if he were running in molasses.

He could hear it scuffling behind him and he was aware of the foul stench of excrement, but still he did not look back. Even as the damp breath was hot on his neck, he stared ahead through bleary eyes. At last the jaws snapped and he felt the pain in his back. He screamed and flapped his arms, and the beast fell from him, the claws raking his skin. Again he yelled, but this time there was no sound. He fell to his knees, tried to rise, but the beast was on him. He tried to curl into a ball to protect himself, but it was snuffling at his belly and his groin, the jawbone sharp, the breath stinking so that he almost gagged with the smell.

He tried to keep his eyes closed, but he could not help but watch as he fought for his life. There was no flesh or fur on the bones, just a skeleton and a skull. He grabbed at the jawbone, trying to force it shut, but it was too strong for him. He felt his life ooze away into the dust and watched the claws dig into him, saw the jawbone snap on his penis. . . .

He awoke screaming.

"Andrew!" The Ambassador's wife had her arms around him, trying to force him back onto the pillow. He fought for a moment, then turned and gazed into her anxious face. Then he shuddered and lay back, drawing the sheet to his chin.

"Are you all right?"

He nodded and tried to speak, but could manage only a whispered affirmative.

"I think you should see the doctor. . . ."

"No." He shook his head violently, then tried to smile, but the expression was distorted into a sneer. "It's okay. I'm fine. Sorry. Go to sleep."

She frowned at him and did as he asked, turning onto her side away from him and closing her eyes. He waited until her breathing was heavy before slipping from the bed. As he tiptoed naked from the bed, he clutched at his torn stomach. He could never tell her. She had always been attracted by his strengths and could not suffer weakness. If he tried to tell her, she would think that he was insane.

He stepped into the shower and turned on the

spray, watching as the blood trickled down his legs. He could feel the sting of the claws in his back, and he gently touched the wound in his stomach. His penis had gone again. The beast always went for the penis, as if it were some kind of special morsel. He laughed to himself, turned off the shower, stepped out, and pulled on his robe.

When he got back to the bed he pulled back the sheet and grimaced. Where he had lain was a mess of blood and the excrement of the jackal. He hoped that Eileen would lie where she was. It would not do for her to turn over and find herself in such a mess. He covered her with the sheet and quietly left the room. He would go to his study and sleep on the couch. Perhaps it would not attack him on the couch. Maybe it would leave him in peace for the rest of the night.

Normally, the morning stroll through Hyde Park was the most relaxing part of Andrew Doyle's day. It was a welcome relief from the desk, the telexes, and the wearisome contents of the diplomatic bag.

For the past year it had become a feature in his life. Indeed, one of the more prestigious magazines had written a piece about it: "A Day in the Life of a United States Ambassador." He remembered how angry the Secret Service had been when the article appeared. They grumbled that publishing the exact time and route of his constitutional made their job more difficult. But then they were always complaining about something.

He looked ahead of him, along the pathway on the north side of the Serpentine. One of his security men was twenty yards in front. Another would be twenty yards behind. He smiled to himself, thinking back. When he had first reached the status when bodyguards became essential, he had been flattered and amused, then later, slightly irritated by the inconvenience.

It had not taken long for him to become so accustomed to their presence that he did not notice them. But now, when he needed them, they were impotent to help. They did not deal in nightmares or hallucinations. If he told them, they would think he was insane.

The dog stood staring along the path, a massive dog, the size of a small pony. Black with a heavy jaw and yellow eyes, it stood motionless, waiting. There was no collar, no sign of an owner. It stood unblinking, the paws planted squarely. Other dogs kept clear of it, and no child came near to pester it. It waited until it saw what it had come for, lifted its head, and stalked up the incline, leaving no marks, and vanished into the bushes.

Doyle walked slowly, looking around him at the activity in the park. He smiled at the gray squirrels scurrying up the beech trees and posing in front of the tourists, demanding nuts. A group of Japanese swarmed around a statue taking pictures of one another. Two men on higher ground to his right were felling a dead elm tree with a chain saw.

Without warning he turned and stared back along the path, turning so unexpectedly that a small boy bumped into him.

"Watch it, mister."

He took no notice. Children were walking in a line past an old woman who was feeding the ducks from a plastic bag. He sighed, shook his head, and resumed his walk.

He closed his eyes for a moment, and when he opened them, he could no longer see the security man in front. The park seemed to have emptied. He shivered as a breeze sprang from nowhere, causing the branches to whip and creak. He looked to his right, up the incline into the bushes, thinking he heard footsteps, but he could see nothing.

He began to move faster, fighting the panic and the urge to run, but he could hear it now behind him, the snuffling and the grunting. Soon he would be able to smell the foul breath.

"God help me," he whispered. The wind was stronger now and he hunched his shoulders, moving painfully forward. He could not look back. He had never looked back. If he turned, he would stare into the terrors of his imagination, and he could not bear to do so.

"Please God," he murmured and began to run, his feet heavy as if he were plowing through mud. As if in answer to his prayer, he turned a bend in the path and saw, fifteen yards ahead, a painted van and a fat salesman smiling at him. Doyle slowed to a walk and made his way purposefully toward it, smoothing back his hair and fixing a smile. He would buy himself a hamburger. He had not eaten one since he was a student, but he could remember the taste of them. They were awful, but he would have one, with mustard and ketchup and onions, and to hell with the smell and to hell with his visitors. They would be too diplomatic to complain.

As he gave his order, he was relieved to find that his voice was steady.

"Just a moment, guv," said the salesman, bending behind the counter, scrabbling for a box of buns. Doyle turned away, looking up into the bushes, thinking of mustard and ketchup, wondering whether he dared have the onions, thinking what they would do to his ulcer.

He turned. The van had gone. All he could see was the dead skull staring at him through sightless eyes, and he could smell sour breath.

"Oh Jesus." He staggered back, stumbled, turned, and ran, his dignity forgotten, back the way he had come, heedless of the shouts of the salesman. The man watched him go, pushed the dog's paws from the counter and cursed at it. He watched it pad soundlessly up the slope, then shrugged his shoulders and threw the bun back into the box.

No longer was Andrew Doyle aware of the people in the park. All he could see was the tableaux of his imagination; predators with canine teeth, scavengers gnawing at the entrails of living things.

Hyenas.

Vultures.

Jackals.

He was out of breath when he reached his limousine, but he did not stop. Ignoring the salute of his chauffeur, he stumbled toward Park Lane, where the traffic was moving fast, heading in three lanes north toward Marble Arch; cars, trucks, taxis, and tourist buses, each one competing as if the road were a race track. Without hesitation, Doyle stepped into the flow, oblivious to the screeching brakes and the yells of anger. He reached the barrier unscathed, clambered over it, and marched blindly into the southbound traffic, squeezing between the fenders until he reached the pavement, then ran toward the Dorchester and through the back streets to Grosvenor Square.

At the embassy he rushed up the steps and burst through the doors past the security men, ignoring their greeting. At his office he moved quickly past his secretary's desk. She smiled at him, stood to give him his messages, but if he heard her he paid no attention. He pushed the double doors open, closed them behind him, leaned back, breathing heavily, and closed his eyes.

When he opened them again he was calmer. The sight of the vast ebony desk, the seal of the United States on the wall, the two furled flags, seemed to compose him. He was back where he belonged.

Gradually his breathing returned to normal, and he made his way to his lavatory. He counted to fifty, ran his hands through his hair, and pressed his thumbs against his temples, his self-control returning. Crooning gently to himself, he turned on the cold tap, cupped his hands, and splashed water on his face, then reached for the towel and glanced at the mirror.

His nightmare stared back at him in the shape of a beast.

Slowly he backed away, his eyes open, staring, then turned his face away from the specter in the mirror, the skull of a scavenger, veins pulsing in the blind, empty eyesockets.

And now he knew that there was nowhere to hide.

Slowly and stiffly he made his way back into the office. For a full minute he stood by his desk, staring at the wall, then reached across the desk and snapped a button on his intercom.

Immediately a voice crackled into the room.

"Press Office."

"This is the Ambassador." His voice was flat and lifeless. "I want to hold a press conference in my office at three o'clock."

"But Mr. Ambassador, you already have a conference scheduled for tomorrow at ten."

Doyle gazed at the Great Seal behind the desk and smoothed back his hair.

"Mr. Ambassador?"

"Three o'clock in my office," he repeated and switched off the machine. He sat at his desk staring into space, then reached into one of the drawers and pulled out a pistol. He blinked as he looked at it, held it up, and gazed down into the barrel. His lips moved in a silent prayer, then he placed the gun on the desk, took the casing from his typewriter, and removed the ribbon. That done, he stood up and moved to the door, unraveling the ribbon as he went. Carefully he wound it around the two handles of the big double door, then methodically walked back to his desk. He looked at the gun, sat down, and glanced at his watch.

Soon there would be no more nightmares.

Kate Reynolds paid off the taxi and made for the steps of the embassy. She was glad to be out of the cab. The driver had been a talker; he had recognized her from the television, called her Katie with the assumed familiarity of the TV viewer. Another five minutes and he would have asked her out to dinner.

She showed her press card at the reception desk and was taken upstairs to the Ambassador's offices. At the door to the reception area she signed the book—Kate Reynolds, BBC—and was ushered inside.

She recognized most of the others, the diplomatic corps from the National Press, a reporter from ITN, and her own crew standing by the window. There was an air of expectancy in the room, each reporter wondering what was going on. It was unheard of to call a press conference on such short notice, especially as there was no running story, nothing obvious to be announced. Like the others, Kate Reynolds was itching with professional curiosity and moved forward toward the big double doors as a secretary announced that the Ambassador would see them now.

Kate was close behind the woman as she tugged at the doors. They stuck for a moment as if jammed. She pulled harder. The doors opened, and Kate glimpsed the typewriter ribbon tied to the handles inside, snaking across the carpet to the desk where the Ambassador was sitting, a gun wedged between his knees.

As the ribbon sprang taut, Kate gasped, heard the explosion, and saw the Ambassador's body lift from the chair as if jerked by ropes, his head snapping backward, half his face shattered, the wall behind him sprayed with blood. Her knees buckled, but still she gazed at the sight as Doyle slumped forward again, his left leg twitching, one eye staring at them, the other smashed beyond recognition by the impact of the heavy bullet. Behind him, parts of his skull made obscene tracks through the blood which obscured the Great Seal.

And still his body moved. Kate remained transfixed as the others around her groaned and shuddered; and before the numbness clouded her mind, she thought that it was a terribly sadistic way for a man to commit suicide.

4
***

The death of Andrew Doyle was bizarre enough to invite all manner of theories, and there was no lack of theorists. His staff was remorsely interrogated. One newspaper suggested that a terrorist organization had sneaked a man into the room, drugged the Ambassador, and attached the typewriter ribbon to the pistol. Other ideas were even more unlikely. If, as had happened a few years ago, a Bulgarian could be stabbed by a poisoned umbrella in the heart of London, they argued, then anything was possible.

Others looked into his background and found no clues. The Ambassador was nearing the end of a long diplomatic career and was due a well-paid retirement. His marriage was sound. There were no skeletons in his closet. If anyone in the world had no reason to kill himself, it was Andrew Doyle; nor did his wife offer any explanation. She said nothing about his screams in the night, and when she looked for reasons to blame herself, searching for guilt, thinking how she could have helped, she could find none. She was as mystified as the rest.

At the moment when Doyle's body was being loaded onto the Washington flight for burial in the capital, Damien Thorn was standing by the desk in the Oval Office of the White House, relaxed and comfortable, waiting for the President of the United States to finish a phone conversation.

He touched the desk with his fingertips, conscious of the fact that he stood near the very apex of political power. From the White House Kennedy had called Khrushchev's bluff over Cuba, here Nixon had gone down on his knees in tears with Kissinger and prayed, Carter had agonized over the hostages in Tehran. But none of these men had been forced to contend with the problems of the present holder of the office. Pick any country, he had once said, and you will find trouble. If there was not direct revolution or internal strife, then there were indirect problems caused by others. Arabs were killing one another in London and Paris. NATO was crumbling, with effects being felt even in the normally placid Scandinavian countries. From Belfast to Tehran, Miami to Kabul, the guns were out and the mops for the blood.

As always, the Middle East was in regular turmoil. People were growing old too quickly just from the strain of holding their breath. And now the dam had burst, quite literally, and the consequences were terrifying.

Damien felt at ease in the office, comfortable, as if he belonged there. He glanced through the window into the Rose Garden, then turned and gazed at the portrait of John F. Kennedy. Some television and newspaper commentators had likened Damien to the Kennedys and to Robert in particular.

Certainly there was a resemblance. Damien was darker than Robert Kennedy but there were the same boyish good looks and the charm which appealed to both men and women. Robert Kennedy could have had his pick of women of his time, and so too could Damien, if he had wished. Both men were rich and powerful in their own right before entering public life. Kennedy's career was legend. Now it was Damien's turn.

He turned and looked at the President, who shrugged at him, as if apologizing for taking so long.

". . . I know that," the President was saying in an exasperated tone. "But I'm not giving out any statements to him or anyone else. It will only make matters worse." He drummed his fingers on the desk. "And make sure the cable is noncommittal: 'The President conveys his condolences, etcetera.' Let me see it before you send it."

He hung up and leaned back in his chair, a portly, weary man who had gone white-haired during the past six months.

"Can you believe that?" he said, looking up at Damien. "The Egyptian opposition wants us to endorse its condemnation of Israel for blowing up the Aswan Dam." He shook his head in disbelief. "How the hell do we know that Israel was responsible?"

Damien shrugged in agreement. "My guess is that it's the work of the NLF," he said.

The president looked blankly back at him. As with some of his predecessors, foreign policy was not his strongest point.

"The Nubian Liberation Front," Damien continued. "They're a quasi-Marxist outfit who have had a gripe against Cairo ever since the dam was built. They claim it submerged fifty percent of their homeland, which of course it did, until now."

Damien continued slowly. "You will remember, sir, when the dam was being constructed there was a massive rescue operation of priceless statues."

"Ah yes," said the President dubiously.

"Rameses the Second?" Damien prompted. "It was a great success as far as the archaeologists were concerned, but it did not help a hundred thousand Nubians who were made homeless."

"There was a United Nations appeal, was there not?" the President said.

"That's right, sir."

The President leaned forward, squinting upward. "How did you get this information?"

Damien looked beyond him into the garden. "One of our relief teams," he said. "They were on the scene before any of the Egyptian rescue units. They've already pieced together a good deal of information from local contacts."

"I'd like to see their report."

"It's quite unofficial, you understand."

The President nodded. "I need hardly point out," he said, "that if we can prove that it had nothing to do with Israel, we could avert a major flareup."

Damien paused as if considering the implications. "I'll have to check it out first myself," he said. "I wouldn't want to feed false information to the White House."

He turned away and gazed once more at the Kennedy portrait.

"As to the other matter," he said carefully, "I'm afraid I can't accept the post. If I were Ambassador to

Great Britain, I'd have to relinquish my control over Thorn, and I—"

"Hell no," said the President, interrupting him. "We can take care of that."

Damien looked at him, feigning surprise. "It's against the law . . ."

The President smiled. He appreciated Damien's gesture. No one would object to the post. Damien, after all, was recognized as one of the most charitable men in the world. If there were any objection it would be dismissed as hair-splitting. No one with any degree of reality would complain. Still, it was good of him to bring it up.

"We'll just have to bend the law," said the President in a tone which suggested that the conversation was at an end. But Damien was not finished.

"There are two other conditions," he said, gazing intently into the President's eyes.

"Try me."

The President fought to control a self-satisfied smirk. So, he was going to take it. At long last the young Thorn was coming in from the political cold. He had been wooed for years by both parties, but now he was going to take sides. Surely now the Democratic coffers would fill up with Thorn contributions.

"First, it could be for only two years, until the Senate race in 'eighty-four."

The President nodded. He had anticipated such a request.

"Second, I want the presidency of the Youth Council."

The President frowned. He hadn't bargained for this. Why on earth did he want such a post? Then he remembered. Damien was forever making speeches

36

about the young. It was almost an obsession, and no one was sure how it had come about. Perhaps it was a result of his background, his father being killed in such horrific and traumatic circumstances when the boy was only six; then his uncle, who had raised him, had disappeared. It must have left a scar. Maybe one day when they were better acquainted he would ask him. Meanwhile the request had made things awkward.

He looked up and shook his head. "I've already promised that post to Foster," he said.

"I realize it's a problem," said Damien, continuing to stare at the other man. For a moment the President held his gaze, then looked away, reaching for a notepad. In that instant Damien knew he had won.

"The NL what?" he asked.

"F," said Damien. "Nubian Liberation Front."

The President made a note, then flicked a switch on his intercom.

"Sandra," he said, talking into the machine. "Send in Craig, will you?" He was about to switch off, then remembered something else. "Oh, and Sandra, don't forget we'll be going to Saturday's ballgame." He glanced up at Damien. "Want to come with Judy and the kids to the ballgame Saturday?"

Damien shook his head. "Sorry, I'm tied up all day."

As the President switched off the intercom, there was a light knock on the door and a young man came in and stood at the door, waiting for permission to move further.

"Craig." The President beckoned him inside, a fresh young man in a sober suit, a neat scrubbed face. "Craig, I'd like you to meet our new Ambassador to the Court of St. James—Damien Thorn."

37

The young man reached out his hand and offered his congratulations.

"Have Eisenberg prepare a press release to that effect, will you?"

"Right away, Mr. President."

The young man turned to go, and Damien turned to the President, frowning slightly.

"Oh yes, and Craig," the President said. "Can you add that Mr. Thorn has also been appointed president of the United Nations Youth Council."

Craig turned, looking surprised. "But I thought—"

"Just do it," said the President irritably.

"Of course, Mr. President."

The President watched the man go, waited until the door was shut, then turned to Damien, his famous smile in place, the smile seen so often on television when he talked to the nation, the smile that widened whenever there was trouble. He eased himself out of his chair and held out his hand.

"Your father would have been very proud of you, Damien."

He was about to elaborate, to say that his father had been one of the most efficient and respected ambassadors to Great Britain, that Robert Thorn would have been pleased by the posting, that perhaps in some way it atoned for the dreadful manner of his death. But Damien cut him short.

"I appreciate your sentiments sir," he said, shaking the older man's hand.

They smiled at one another, and the President felt an involuntary shiver run down his spine. The man was so self-assured. It was as if this were Damien's office and he, the President, were the visitor. And as he watched him leave, he realized that Damien had not mentioned Andrew Doyle. Everyone else had expressed shock and disbelief and had offered condolences. But from Damien there was not a word. It was as if the ex-Ambassador had never existed.

5

***

Harvey Dean looked up and winked at the stewardess who was leaning over him, telling him that it was okay to unfasten his seat belt. He ordered a martini, leaned back in his seat, and glanced across at Damien sitting next to him, engrossed in a novel.

He reached for his briefcase and felt at peace with himself. Normally he was not one to indulge in self-analysis, but very occasionally he looked back on his life and marveled at how far he had come. This was one such occasion, sitting in a Thorn jet heading for London, in an aircraft powerful enough to whip them across the Atlantic and luxurious enough to convince the passengers that they were already settled in the Savoy on the Strand.

He took his martini, thanked the stewardess, and sipped it. The cocktail was exactly as he liked it: extra dry, all gin, the vermouth bottle turned toward Paris as a gesture.

Dean considered himself fortunate. He knew his strengths and his weaknesses, a self-knowledge that in itself was one of his major strengths. One weakness was his inability to understand people. His view of human nature was blinkered, and he was often unsure of motives, constantly surprised by the reactions of other human beings. But he could fillet a balance sheet for essentials in seconds. He had a natural grasp of the workings of the business world, a prophetic eye for the main chance, and he could spot trouble before it had begun to brew.

It was these qualities which had taken him from the obscurity of the Harvard Business School eight years earlier and into the boardroom of the biggest multinational conglomerate in the world.

Even now he could recall every detail of his first meeting with Paul Buher. Dean had accepted the lunch invitation graciously and had gone along to the restaurant itching with curiosity.

Buher had come straight to the point. A number of Thorn executives had been impressed with a course that Dean had run at Harvard. Buher had seen his file and had also been impressed, enough, as president of the corporation, to make him an offer personally.

Dean was flattered, and he accepted the post before the main course was served. He was fascinated by Buher from the start. He had heard much about him, how ruthless he was. He knew that it was Buher who, some twelve years previously, had persuaded Thorn Industries to diversify, to go into fertilizers and soya, a decision which had turned Thorn from a mere giant of industry to a multinational colossus. It was Buher who had realized that the people who controlled the foodstuffs made the bread.

By the second brandy, Dean had felt confident

enough to ask if it was true that Buher had once said the line which had become famous: "Our profitable future lies in just one thing . . . famine!"

And Buher had shrugged. "Something like that, I believe."

A month later, Dean had become a Thorn employee. Two weekends later, Buher began the process of changing his life. There was a weekend party at Buher's country residence. Barbara, Dean's wife, was spending the summer months in the Hamptons, and it was the traditional time for the men of the Eastern Seaboard, at work in the cities, to acquire mistresses and mysteries.

The woman whom Buher introduced to Dean was named Ayesha. She was, she told him, half Venezuelan and part Creole, and Dean, who had spent most of his life sheltered behind the walls of colleges, had met no one like her.

Dean was staggered by the sexual appetites of the woman. It was something he had never experienced, a rough initiation, a sexuality which, in his more naive days, he would have dismissed as perverse. It involved a lot of pain.

After the second night she had produced a Bible. At first, Dean had thought the book was a prop, another bizarre fantasy, but she was serious as she schooled him in the secrets within its pages; and in his ecstasy, his mind and body dazzled by the drugs she fed him and the oils she used on him, it began to make sense. She did her job so well that when he was told who Damien Thorn really was, he could have cried for joy.

Since that day he had been prepared to follow Damien to the ends of the earth and would gladly die for him if necessary. And to his surprise he found it easy to keep the secret from Barbara.

He reached into his briefcase for his papers, found the ones he wanted, and laid the case by his side.

"The Soviet Union is offering Egypt soya at fifty dollars a ton on a five-year loan at seven and a half percent," he said. "That's eight dollars less than what we're asking. They've got wheat on offer from Canada at ninety-five dollars a ton, corn at eighty-two, but there's no way they can afford it."

"How much soya do we have stockpiled?" Damien asked, without raising his eyes from his book.

"Approximately eight hundred and fifty million tons worldwide."

"All right. Let them have the soya at thirty dollars a ton at five percent over ten years." He looked up for the first time and smiled. "That should put the government in our pocket for the next decade."

Dean made a note on his pad, listening carefully as Damien continued.

"The President is pushing for that NLF report, but I don't want him to have it till it's out of date. How soon can we pin the blame for the dam on Israel?"

"We've got a disciple in Tel Aviv, name of Schroeder," said Dean. "Under Secretary for Defense in the Israeli government. Buher talked to him last night, and Schroeder says he can forge the necessary documents to implicate them up to the hilt."

Damien glanced at him sharply. "No way of tracing it back to us?" he asked.

"Buher says not," said Dean, aware that he was passing the buck and content to do so.

"Okay," said Damien. "How long will it take him?"

"Couple of weeks at the most."

"Fine."

43

Damien returned to his book and Dean to his work. As the plane leveled out, Damien looked up again.

"When is Barbara coming over?"

"She should be in London by the weekend. It's a five-day sea crossing. I tried to persuade her to come with us, but she didn't want to run the risk of having the baby in midflight."

Damien grinned. "I can't think of a better place to be born."

Dean chuckled and picked up a financial report. For the rest of the flight they sat in silence, each man relaxing in his own manner.

It would be an easy flight, the captain informed them over the speaker. There was a tailwind and the skies over London were clear and welcoming.

As the Thorn jet was circling Heathrow Airport, Father De Carlo, in Subiaco, was gathering his monks around him.

One by one they filed into the dark crypt beneath the monastery, their heads bowed, arms crossed within the folds of their cassocks. When the last man had entered, Father De Carlo raised his hands and they knelt before him in a semicircle, gazing up at the cross and at the little tabernacle beside it.

Father De Carlo reached for the massive Bible under the cross, turned to the Book of Revelation, and began to read:

" 'And there appeared a great wonder in heaven; a woman clothed with the sun, and the moon under her feet, and upon her head a crown of twelve stars.

" 'And she being with child cried, travailing in birth, and pained to be delivered.

" 'And there appeared another wonder in heaven;

and behold a great red dragon, having seven heads and ten horns, and seven crowns upon his heads.

" 'And his tail drew the third part of the stars of heaven, and did cast them to the earth; and the dragon stood before the woman which was ready to be delivered, for to devour her child as soon as it was born.

" 'And she brought forward a man child, who was to rule all nations with a rod of iron; and her child was caught up unto God, and to His throne.

" 'And the woman fled into the wilderness where she hath a place prepared of God . . .' "

He bowed his head in silent prayer, then turned to the tabernacle as the monks chanted a response. He opened the doors, took out the pouch, and arranged the daggers in a semicircle at the foot of the cross, the blades pointing outward; a ring of protective steel.

As the chant came to an end, he knelt before the altar. Briefly there was silence in the crypt.

"O Blessed Savior," he whispered, "who hath, through the confessions of Thy departed servant, Father Spilletto, revealed unto us the identity of the Anti-Christ here on earth, grant us Thy strength and guidance in our holy mission that we may rid the world of Damien Thorn, and thus ensure the sanctity of Thy second coming."

He spread his hands over the daggers.

"O Lord, bless these seven sacred knives of Megiddo, which Thou hast seen fit to return to us, that they may serve their holy purpose and destroy the Prince of Darkness, even as he seeketh to destroy the Child of Light."

The monks whispered, "Amen," as Father De Carlo slowly rose to his feet and turned to them.

"I now call upon each of you to come forward and arm yourselves in the name of the Lord.

"Brother Martin."

A small man got to his feet. He was bald with a bright nervous face. He stepped forward, took one of the daggers, grasped it firmly, and backed away.

"Brother Paolo." The black monk took his place.

"Brother Simeon." The youngest of the group; boyishly handsome.

"Brother Antonio." A powerful man, with a full gray beard and a mass of hair.

"Brother Matteus." A gentle-looking man in his forties, quiet and unassuming.

"Brother Benito." Young and dark, with an intense expression as if he carried the woes of the world on his shoulders.

There was a single dagger left. Father De Carlo picked it up and looked into the face of each of the monks.

"Before setting out from this place," he said, "each of us must pray to our Lord in the silence of his own soul."

Silently they turned and made their way out of the crypt, up the worn flagstones to their cells. They crossed the hallway and moved into the corridor. In silence they entered their cells; bare rooms, just a bed, a table, and a pitcher. Each monk kneeled by his bed, eyes closed in prayer, the dagger held like a crucifix.

Below, in the crypt, Father De Carlo prayed for all of them.

"Since we are prepared to lay down our lives in the pursuit of this enterprise, we must seek final absolution now, lest we be denied the redemption of the blessed last sacrament at the moment of death."

As one man, each of the monks shuddered and clutched the dagger to his chest.

"Above all, we must ask God to grant us courage,

guidance, and strength as we prepare to do battle with Satan and his son, the Anti-Christ.

"The exact hour of our Lord's Second Coming, for which we have wept for centuries, has now been revealed to us by signs in the heavens. It is imperative that the destruction of the Anti-Christ take place before then, and we have but a short time in which to carry it out."

He gazed upward, seeing nothing. His mind held a vision of the future, and he grasped at it.

"My brothers, remember that these seven daggers and ourselves are all that stands between the Son of Satan and the Son of God, for they alone can destroy him."

He rose to his feet and stared at the cross, thinking of Robert Thorn, the man whose baby had been murdered at birth to make way for the Anti-Christ, the skull of Thorn's child crushed by a stone and the monster, born of a jackal impregnated by the Devil, put in its place. He remembered as a novice monk taking the confession of Father Spilletto, who had assisted at the blasphemous birth. It had been too terrible to imagine.

He offered up a short prayer for the soul of Thorn, who had brought up the Anti-Christ, who, in return, had murdered Thorn's wife, his unborn second baby, and others who posed a threat to him; Robert Thorn, dead of a policeman's bullet, even as he tried to rid the world of the Satanic child.

Then there was Robert's brother, Richard, who, in his ignorance, had raised the child to puberty and who had vanished with his wife from the face of the earth: Richard and Ann Thorn and so many others.

There had been so many deaths, so many innocent victims. But this time, there could be no failure, for the fate of the world depended on them, a priest and six monks, men of peace, gentle souls trained to be passive, meditative, contemplative. And now they were being asked to commit a terrible violence, to go against their natures, to turn their plowshares back into swords.

He could never have foreseen such a thing, not as a young man in Milan when he had first made his vows, not in all the years as a novice, not even when he became a priest; all that he had wanted was to serve God, to contemplate His goodness and to promote His kingdom on earth. Yet he, De Carlo, had at least traveled the world. He had been on an airplane. He had attended seminars out of the country. He had seen the ways of men. At least he knew something of the world. But the others . . .

He thought of each one of them and his eyes filled with tears.

6

For the embassy reception Kate Reynolds chose the Chloé cocktail dress—calf-length, somber, elegant, and very expensive-looking. She had managed to steal an hour for the hairdresser and now was ready for the evening. She wore a minimum of makeup. Men had told her she did not need any cosmetic help. She had a strong face, high cheekbones, wide eyes, a classic profile. As she ducked into the cab, she decided that she would not disgrace the BBC. She waved to her son, who was standing by the door, and he bowed cheekily toward her. He had called her well preserved for her age, and from Peter, that was a compliment.

She told the driver to head for the American Embassy. It was the second time that month. As the cab eased its way through the streets, she saw again in her mind the blasted skull of Andrew Doyle, and she shuddered at the memory.

No one had come up with an answer to the mystery of the suicide. No one who knew Doyle could offer any clue. It was as unexpected as it was bizarre, and now the new Ambassador had moved in quickly, almost too quickly, installed in the office before the new paint on the Great Seal was completely dry.

Kate was more than curious about Damien Thorn. At thirty-two he was awfully young for the important job, but it was no secret that he was merely using it as the first step on the political ladder. She grimaced as she recalled the phone call that afternoon to the correspondent in Washington. The man had leered at her across the transatlantic cable, telling her how handsome Thorn was, how charming, how she would enjoy interviewing him—the old tired smut of an old tired man.

The fact that Thorn was not married interested her. There were duties for an ambassador's wife to perform, and it would be interesting to see who would fill the role. But there was no regular woman in his life; nor had there been any hint of a scandal. Thirty-two and unmarried—the inevitable doubt rose to mind and was quickly submerged. Not even the progressive Americans would send a gay ambassador to London—which was just as well, Kate thought wryly. The city seemed to be crawling with ancient homosexual spies, popping out of the woodwork and the Sunday papers every couple of weeks. . . . She scolded herself for her unruly imagination and reached for her purse as the cab turned into Grosvenor Square.

The reception room was paneled in oak, the walls hung with dark portraits in oil. Gold-framed mirrors reached to the ceiling; the drapes were deep velvet and heavy; a massive chandelier lit the room. The place reeked, she thought, of extravagance.

Automatically she checked the guest list as she presented her invitation. Very few other journalists had been invited, just the diplomatic writers from the serious papers. Briefly she wondered if there was any gossip for the *Mail* and *Express*. Maybe they would try to gate-crash, or, failing that, they would be buying tidbits from the waiters or cornering the younger diplomats later at Tramp or Morton's.

She knew exactly why she had been picked for the occasion. She had formally asked the embassy if Damien Thorn would appear on her program. The request was being considered, and now she had the opportunity to approach him personally and perhaps charm him.

Gazing around, she picked up a glass of wine and snippets of conversation. It was the normal trivia of the early evening; sports, the weather, nothing serious or controversial.

To her right she spotted two elderly men and recognized them as Foreign Office, veterans of such gatherings. They leaned against one another, completely at home, one of them examining the label of the wine bottle.

"Lafite Thorn," he mused in a voice marinated in claret.

"Bought the bugger out," wheezed the other.

"Amazing what they can produce from soya beans these days."

Kate smiled at them and moved across. "Is he really only thirty-two?" she asked, happily butting into their conversation.

"No idea," shrugged the wheezer. "Shouldn't be surprised. Americans always seem to think they can run before they can walk." He sniffed. "Like their wine."

"To answer your question," murmured a voice behind her, "yes, he is. The youngest ambassador ever appointed by the President."

Kate turned to see a dapper, bespectacled man smiling at her.

"Harvey Dean," he said. "Private secretary to the Ambassador."

Kate shook hands and introduced herself.

"My wife, Barbara," said Dean.

Again Kate shook hands. Barbara was a pleasant-looking woman, slightly gauche and, in a room like this, totally out of place. She was also very pregnant and happy to talk about it. Kate could not think of a single thing to say to her.

"Would you care to meet the Ambassador?" asked Dean.

"Very much." That, after all, was what she was here for, not to exchange knitting patterns with the secretary's wife. She had already spotted Damien across the room, and instantly she had been aware of the man's appeal. Charm plus looks plus, presumably, intelligence. What else? she wondered. What about the minuses?

She followed Dean through the throng of guests. Damien stood by the fireplace, his profile reflected in the mirror above it. Gently touching elbows, Dean insinuated her into the group and attracted Damien's attention.

"Mr. Ambassador," he said, "this is Kate Reynolds of the BBC. Miss Reynolds hosts her own weekly news show, *The World in Vision*."

"*World in Focus*," said Kate.

"Sorry, *in Focus*," said Dean.

"Or out of," said Kate, "as the case may be."

Damien bowed slightly. "Pleased to meet you, Miss

Reynolds. You are the Barbara Walters of the BBC, perhaps?"

Kate shook her head. "On my salary? We're not called the British Broadcasting Charity for nothing, you know."

Damien's smile widened, and he moved closer, telling her in mock confidentiality that he was also in the charity business. Kate gave herself top marks. She was hardly in the room and already she and the Ambassador were chattering like old friends. One up for Chloé, she thought. She decided to ride her luck. "Are you enjoying London?"

"I expect I shall," said Damien. "Everything I have seen so far is very attractive."

Kate smiled, accepting the compliment.

"You do know that I have asked to see you. Officially, that is."

"I hadn't heard," Damien said. "What would you like to discuss?"

"I'd like to hear more about your views on youth," she said. "My son, Peter, is a great fan of yours. He's only twelve but he seems to think you have all the right ideas—"

She was interrupted by Dean, leaning between them. The Israeli Ambassador was leaving and wanted a word . . .

Damien took her hand. "I'd be happy to talk to you," he said. "Give Harvey a ring tomorrow and he'll arrange a time. How about Sunday?"

Of course, she thought. But there was Peter to think about. Sunday was the only day they spent together. Normally it was sacrosanct. She was caught in that instant between two conflicting duties. Immediately Damien solved the problem.

"Bring Peter along too," he said.

Kate watched him cross the room. She took another glass from a tray and congratulated herself. It was remarkable. Too easy. Almost too good to be true.

Charm, looks, intelligence.

And no wife.

From the beginning, Peter and Damien were firm friends. So much so that Kate had to fight off a twinge of irrational jealousy. Again she was surprised by Damien, for never before had Peter taken to a man so quickly. Normally he was silent or cutting, either excessively polite or quietly rude. But with Damien he was himself, excitable and charming, as if he had known the man all his life.

As she watched them together, that following Sunday in Hyde Park, the two of them kneeling by the Serpentine, playing with a model speedboat, she was struck by her son's vitality. He was twelve now and becoming very handsome, taking after his father.

His grandmother had said sweet old-fashioned things about him; that he would leave a trail of broken hearts. A colleague from the BBC, a reporter in his forties, had been more direct. He had said that Peter was beautiful, as simple as that, and since then Kate had managed to keep the boy away from him.

She reached into her bag, took out her camera, and glanced through the viewfinder. Damien and Peter were bent at the water's edge and did not see the camera, but then a strange large dog came up to gaze at her, and Kate involuntarily stepped back from its glare. Instinctively she was frightened of it. The beast was so big and black, with its massive jaw and dreadful eyes tinged with yellow.

She tried to ignore it, pressed the button, put the

camera away, and moved toward them, hearing Peter ask to work the controls of the model boat.

Briefly Kate wondered if Damien was playing the old game—make a fuss of the child in order to get to the woman—but she dismissed the thought. He was not crass enough for that, and besides, he had no need.

"Hey, Mummy!" Peter rose to his feet as she approached, his eyes gleaming. He was holding the controls of the boat in his hand. "Look what Damien's given me! And I didn't ask him for it, I swear."

Kate shook her head and turned to Damien. The boat was far too expensive.

"Oh, but you can't," she said.

"Oh, but he can," Peter mimicked her. "He just did."

Damien looked at Kate. "It will be much safer with him," he said. "If I were to collide with another ship, it could spark a major international crisis."

And there was nothing more to be said.

Together they watched Peter with his new acquisition.

"You shouldn't spoil him," said Kate.

"Kids deserve to get spoiled now and then."

"I know. I do it all the time. My husband died when Peter was a baby." She did not know why she was telling him this, unsolicited, but she continued, "So you can imagine how he twists me around his little finger."

"To tell the truth, he's the one who's been spoiling me," said Damien. "It isn't every day I get the chance to be a boy again. You must be very proud of him. I would be if I had a son like him."

"I am," Kate said. "But don't tell him. He's conceited enough as it is."

She looked up at him and put the obvious question. "Have you ever thought of getting married?"

Damien shook his head. "I'm too much of a skeptic. Besides, I haven't had the time."

"What's the hurry?"

Damien shrugged, watching Peter with the boat. "You know, sometimes I really wonder." For a moment he stood in silence, then turned and looked down at the dog, which had come up to gaze back at him, its eyes narrowing, a gaze of apparent disapproval.

"Peter's always at me to buy him a dog," said Kate.

"You should do so." Damien continued to stare at the persistent beast. "Boys and dogs go great together. We've had a dog like that in the family ever since I was a kid. They marched with the Roman army, you know, two thousand years ago."

"Really?"

"They're as old as sin."

The dog rose and padded away. Damien and Kate followed, and Peter trailed behind them, carrying the boat and occasionally throwing sticks for the dog. To the casual observer they were a perfect family group, strolling east through the park.

As they left the Serpentine, Kate remembered that this was the same route Andrew Doyle had taken on the day he died. She mentioned it briefly, saying how sorry she was, but if Damien had heard he paid no attention, and she shrugged, assuming his mind was elsewhere.

When they reached the Speakers' Corner, Peter left them and ran toward an ice-cream van. Groups of people clustered around the orators, and the voice of one man rang out clear among the general babble.

" . . 'The day of Christ is at hand,' wrote St. Paul in his Second Letter to the Thessalonians."

Damien and Kate threaded their way through the crowd.

" 'Yet let no man deceive you, for that day shall not come before the Man of Sins be revealed, the Son of Perdition, the Anti-Christ. And be not deceived, for Satan himself is transformed into an angel of light . . .' "

Kate heard the words but did not take them in.

"You must think me very unprofessional, Damien," she said. "I haven't asked you half the questions I meant to."

"That's why it's been such a pleasure," he replied. "You can save the questions for the program."

Good, thought Kate, it was decided. The morning had been more than enjoyable: it had been worthwhile. It had proved productive, professionally speaking. Damien Thorn's first appearance on British television would be on her program.

As she congratulated herself, she realized she was now standing alone. Damien had stopped a few paces behind her and was gazing fixedly forward.

"The hour of Christ's Second Coming draws nigh . . ."

Kate followed his gaze and saw a lay preacher standing on a box, a placard by his side proclaiming that the Second Coming was at hand. She smiled indulgently and walked back to Damien's side.

"The prophecies fulfilled one by one," the preacher continued. " 'And there shall be signs in the sun, and in the moon, and in the stars . . .'

"Right now, my friends, in the constellation of Cassiopeia, a holy trinity of stars is converging to herald our Lord's Second Coming, and as the star over Bethlehem guided the wise men of old, so this trinity will summon forth the faithful to pay homage before Him."

The preacher turned and caught the sight of Damien. Their eyes locked and they stared unblinkingly at one another, oblivious to anyone else.

" 'Rejoice then, you heavens, and see that you dwell in them,' commanded St. John in Revelation. 'But woe to you, earth and sea, for the Devil hath come to you in great fury, knowing that his time is short . . .' "

"What's the matter, Damien?" The boy looked puzzled, seeing the stark expression.

"Nothing." Damien relaxed, looking down at him, accepting the ice cream the boy had bought for him. "I was just marveling at one of your more eccentric British institutions."

Peter nodded and turned to Kate, offering her an ice cream. As he held it up, he saw his mother flinch. Peter turned, startled by her expression, and grinned when he saw that it was only the dog again. It stood stock-still, the paws planted square, its hackles rising, growling deep in its throat.

"Hello, dog," Peter said, holding his hand out to it.

"Peter," said Kate sharply, "stay away from it."

Peter shook his head and whistled to the dog. "It's only you he doesn't like, Mum."

The dog was staring past Kate toward the trees, its eyes fixed on a man standing watching them, a tall man, black as night.

"C'mon, dog," said Peter, snapping his fingers. The dog turned to him, the hackles went down, and it padded across, licked Peter's hand, then moved across to Damien. Kate, keeping well back, turned again to watch the orators, and she did not hear the conversation between her son and Damien.

"I wonder why he doesn't like Mummy."

"Because she's not one of us."

Nor did she see the expression that passed between them.

"'. . . and the Prince of Darkness shall be mighty,'" the preacher continued, "'and he shall prosper, and destroy the mighty, and he shall cause craft to prosper in his hand, and by peace he shall destroy many.'"

The monks had been waiting all afternoon, and Father De Carlo was becoming fidgety. He stood at the window, which was smeared in grease and dust, and he stared up from the basement at the crumbling red brick houses opposite.

He looked up, but the sky was just a gray patch of cloud like a cheap ceiling wallpaper tacked on between the roofs. He shook his head. Cable Street was depressing. The mission they had been guided to was a damp slum. All his life Father De Carlo had lived by his faith and within the strict boundaries of his imagination. The outside world, his physical surroundings, were meant to be irrelevant to him. Yet the East End of London was so depressing it made Subiaco seem like paradise. At least the sun shone in Subiaco and you could see the sky. He felt sorry for those who were forced to live here all their lives.

He glanced at the others as they huddled miserably in the dark room. For each of them it had been a journey of a lifetime. He had felt like a shepherd guiding them through the formalities at the airport, watching them fumble for tickets, their eyes everywhere, trying not to notice the women, standing in a small cluster, stranded as surely as if they were on a desert island. The coffers had been cleaned out to pay for the journey, and there would need to be a good harvest that year if they were not to be reduced to the begging bowl in the winter. Each of them had prayed on the aircraft, then sat in silence in the airport bus as it drove into London.

The mood of the party fluctuated as they traveled through the city. They gasped at the splendor of Mayfair, frowned at the shabbiness of Piccadilly Circus, and shuddered at the bleak brickwork of the East End. When finally their taxis drew up at the mission, they looked at one another, shrugging their shoulders, each one hoping that soon they would be back home.

His thoughts were interrupted by sounds of shuffling on the stairs, and he turned to see Matteus and Paolo enter the room, Matteus holding his placard prophesying the Second Coming. He was flushed with excitement and could not wait to tell his story. Father De Carlo motioned them to join the others. When they were all seated, Father De Carlo let Matteus talk.

They had seen him, he said, that afternoon, not more than ten feet away, with a woman, a child, and a dog, the Anti-Christ in human form.

"Who was the woman?" Father De Carlo asked.

It was Paolo who answered, reaching into his jacket for a notebook. "A television reporter. I asked someone who went up to her for her autograph." He flipped the notebook open. "Kate Reynolds. She's apparently quite a celebrity."

"And the boy?"

Paolo shrugged. "Probably her son."

Father De Carlo leaned forward, resting his elbows on the table; a woman and a child, he thought. What was he up to? But Matteus was forcing his way back into the conversation.

"Please, Father," he implored. "Let me be the one.

Thorn and I made contact—eye to eye. Let me be the bait to flush him out and destroy him."

Father De Carlo shook his head and sighed. They were so impetuous, so brave and naive, so terribly naive.

"He will have read your thoughts as surely as you read his," he said. "We have to strike him off guard."

He glanced around the room, dark and dank even in the light of day; seven men sitting round a creaking table; seven daggers. It seemed such a small, inadequate army to put against such opposition.

"The target must be still for the marksman to be sure of his aim," said one of the monks.

"A sitting target," said another. "Or a sleeping target perhaps."

Father De Carlo shook his head. "His residence is guarded day and night."

"And the embassy?" asked another.

This time Father De Carlo did not bother to reply. It was left to Paolo to mutter, "Impossible." Father De Carlo had seen the building in Grosvenor Square, the imposing size of it, the guards on duty; and this was the place Brother Martin wanted to attack, with his one dagger.

A quiet voice broke through the clouds of his despair. "There's our sitting target."

Father De Carlo looked up at the face of Benito, who pointed to his left past the other monks into the corner, at the broken-down television set, resting on three legs.

At first Father De Carlo did not understand what he was getting at, until Benito and Paolo began to improvise an idea; and from that damp basement in an East End slum Father De Carlo raised his eyes to heaven and thanked God for His inspiration.

7

Brother Benito stood in the drizzle for an hour before he saw what he wanted. He was uncomfortable, unaccustomed to the suit of clothes he had been given. The trousers were tight around his waist and groin, and he could not imagine why people restricted themselves to such clothing. The cassock was so much more sensible. He stood in the doorway of a public house in Shepherd's Bush watching the people go by about their business. The dagger, wrapped in a piece of cloth, lay snugly against his thigh, and he held it through his trouser pocket, caressing the hilt.

The tourist bus had drawn up in front of the studios, and as the passengers filed out, Benito sneaked out of the doorway and surreptitiously joined the end of the line. He smiled at the security guard at the gate and his colleague at the reception desk and within minutes was inside the studio. Ducking away from the tourists, he entered the room marked "Gentlemen," opened the door of a cubicle, and locked it behind him. He was inside, and he prayed that his luck would hold.

He waited until he felt confident enough to leave, then peered out into the corridor. It took him fifteen minutes wandering the building to find a bulletin board which told him his destination, and another ten to find Studio 4. Glancing behind him, he tried the door. It swung open and he slipped inside. The place was empty and dark, but he could see, among the props and the equipment, a number of places to hide. He was through the second-to-last hoop. Now all he had to do was wait until the program began.

Damien arrived forty minutes later. After a brief conversation with Kate and the producer, he was taken to the makeup room, his two security men flanking him, Harvey Dean walking behind him.

As a makeup woman dabbed his face with powder he noticed over her shoulder, reflecting in the mirror, a television monitor showing the opening sequence of *World in Focus*. He watched impassively as the screen filled with crowds of refugees moving distractedly along the banks of a swollen river. The scene shifted to the Aswan Dam, cracked in two places, water flowing through the breach. No one noticed the smile that flickered briefly across Damien's lips.

Kate Reynolds' voice filled the room, relayed through two speakers:

". . . the Israeli government has consistently denied any responsibility for the Aswan Dam disaster, which has so far claimed the lives of over fifty thousand Egyptians, though many fear that the final death toll may reach twice that number.

"Already typhoid has broken out among the countless thousands of homeless refugees swarming the banks of the Nile, and a major epidemic now seems unavoidable."

Damien glanced at the door, where two of the embassy security staff stood idly watching the screen.

"As in Cambodia, the main source of aid has come not through any government or charitable agency, but through the Thorn Corporation of America."

At this, the makeup woman stepped back, flicked a speck of powder off Damien's nose and reached for a hairbrush.

The monitor showed the Thorn Relief Units at work, unloading soya sacks from supply ships and distributing food and medical supplies.

"By the end of this week," said Kate, "they will have distributed over eight million tons of soya produce from their massive stockpiles around the world."

The woman leaned over toward Damien, but he snapped his head away, his hand grabbing her wrist.

"That's okay," he said. "I'll do it myself."

She handed him the brush and leaned back against the dressing table.

In her line of work she had seen vanity in many different manifestations, and here was another. Damien Thorn might be personally feeding half the world's starving population, but he insisted on brushing his own hair. It was curious, but then most of the people who came into her room were curious. Aim a television camera at people and they go peculiar. Like many in her trade, she was observant, and later she confided to a friend that there was something odd about Damien Thorn. His skin seemed coarse, his fingers smooth as if there were no prints, as if he had been in a fire. But she had no means of guessing that

Damien's secret was etched in his scalp, the secret that had led to the death of Robert Thorn all those years ago, and so many before and since.

Damien brushed a stray hair into place and turned to watch the television monitor.

"Although the Thorn Corporation has been criticized by some observers for what the Soviet News Agency, Tass, terms 'the capitalist exploitation of human tragedy,' the Egyptian government has revealed that Thorn is supplying soya at almost fifty percent below the current market price."

The door opened, and a young man looked in and asked Damien if he was ready. Damien nodded, smiled at the makeup woman, and left the room, flanked by his security men.

Kate's voice followed them along the corridor.

"At the center of Thorn's global operation is the man who has become a legend in his own time. . . ."

Damien smiled as he stepped through the studio doors into the darkness. In the distance he saw Kate, bathed in light, sitting demurely, three cameras focused on her face. The floor manager approached, smiling, holding a finger to his lips, then led him forward, the two men stepping gingerly across cables and between idle cameras. They stopped a few feet from the set, and Damien spotted Dean in the shadow. The little man came forward and tapped his watch.

"A half hour here," he said. "Then back to Pereford. Buher is phoning later, then there's the Israeli papers . . ." His voice murmured in a monotone, Dean ticking off points in a mental diary. Without warning he leaned forward and whispered.

"Have you seen the faggots in here? Huh? Amazing, isn't it?"

Damien smiled. Harvey Dean might be forty, but

he retained the sense of wonder of a ten-year-old. The world astonished him. If he lived to be a hundred he could never be blasé.

From the opposite end of the studio, Benito walked slowly forward, his hand on the hilt of the dagger. Perspiration ran down his arms and beaded on his forehead.

"Last week," Kate continued, "Mr. Thorn arrived in Britain to become the youngest ambassador ever appointed to what we still refer to as our Court of St. James, and later in the program I shall be talking to him."

Benito took a deep, deep breath, then stepped back as the floor manager guided Damien toward the set and pointed him toward the guest chair opposite Kate.

"But first," said Kate, "let's take a look at a few of the highlights in a career that's already been compared to that of the late John F. Kennedy. . . ."

Benito calculated the distance as Damien settled himself in the chair. It was ten, maybe twelve, paces. He closed his eyes, murmured a few words of prayer, opened his eyes again, and raised himself onto his toes.

"Can I help you?" The voice in his ear startled him, and he turned to see a man behind him, carrying a clipboard and looking curiously at him.

"What?" said Benito, trying to hide his confusion.

"You're not connected with this program, are you?" It was a challenge rather than a question.

"I'm looking for Studio Eight," said Benito quickly.

"This is Studio Four," the man said as if talking to a child. "Studio Eight is across the corridor."

Benito thanked him and scurried away into the darkness, Kate's voice following him:

"After majoring at Yale University, Damien Thorn attended Oxford as a Rhodes scholar, captaining the

Oxford eight to victory in 1966, as well as winning the Westchester Cup at polo in the same year. . . ."

At the door Benito turned. He could see the man with the clipboard still staring at him. Confused, he moved away from the door toward a stack of lighting equipment. The man stared after him, one hand over his eyes, then turned and whispered to another who had been watching the program. Together the two men peered into the darkness, then began to make their way toward the door.

Benito groaned and moved swiftly to his right, moving blindly, trying to think, wondering what to do, where to hide, what to say when he was found. His shoulder hit something and, looking up, he saw the bottom rung of an iron ladder leading to a lighting gantry. Without thinking he pulled himself up, his rubber soles scrabbling for a grip, and hung like a bat as the two men stood ten feet away from him.

"In 1975," Kate was saying, "Damien took over the reins of his uncle's business, Thorn Industries, and within seven years had turned it into the world's largest multinational corporation, producing everything from nuclear armaments to soya-bean food products. . . ."

The two men peered into the darkness, then shrugged their shoulders and went back toward the set. Benito, his arms aching, hauled himself up the ladder, moving slowly until he reached the lighting gantry. Briefly he paused, then began to creep soundlessly forward.

Kate's voice wafted up to him:

"And now, at the age of thirty-two, Damien Thorn has entered public life, not only as U.S. Ambassador to Britain but as president of the United Nations Youth Council. . . ."

Benito grunted to himself, the nearest he had come to uttering an oath.

"It would not be surprising," Kate continued, "if in a few years' time he might be running for the U. S. Senate, and perhaps even for President."

He could see Kate turn toward Damien, twenty feet beneath him, and he stopped and looked around him, trying to see if he could inch his way any closer so that he could position himself directly above his quarry.

"You've had a remarkable career for one so young," Kate was saying.

"Oh, I don't know," said Damien. "Not when you remember that Alexander the Great was commanding the Macedonian army at sixteen."

Benito snorted in disgust and moved forward, tripping on something. He froze as he saw a loose bolt teeter at the brink of the gantry, then plummet to the floor, bouncing at the feet of one of the crew. Holding his breath, Benito stood motionless, squinting downward. Two men were moving around beneath him, staring upward, but they were blinded by the arc lights and soon they turned away. Again Benito murmured a silent prayer and set off once more, sliding one foot forward and following it with the other, moving only a few inches at a time.

"Many people view you as a sort of twentieth-century Alexander," Kate was saying. "Leading the world out of the present doldrums of recession into a golden era of prosperity."

Damien smiled. "You have been watching too many of my commercials."

"But it is the image you manage to put across," Kate persisted.

"The image of Thorn as a corporation, not a personal image. But I certainly hold tremendous optimism for the future, and I want to see Thorn play a major part in achieving it."

Benito stopped and risked another glance over the gantry, shaking his head as he saw it veer away from the set. He had come so close only to fail. He could not jump. He would break his neck. Fighting back despair, he thought of alternatives. Perhaps, if he waited, he could try the attack when the show was over, catch Damien in one of the corridors, take a chance on getting past the security men. But it was unlikely.

Beneath him lay a set of lighting boats stretching across the studio, suspended some ten feet above the floor. He gazed blankly at them, trying to think what they reminded him of. They were like lifeboats on a ship. He remembered his one trip to sea, and his uncle telling him of a shipwreck years ago when the sailors had scrambled from one sinking lifeboat to another. . . .

Benito pursed his lips and clenched his fists, feeling the adrenaline pump through him once more. If only the chains would hold. He reached out and tugged the nearest one. It seemed secure enough. Looking up, he could see it snake up to the roof. Praying it would hold his weight, he wrapped one leg around the chain, grasped it firmly in both hands, stepped off the gantry, and slithered soundlessly into the boat, where he crouched breathlessly. He felt the dagger dig into his thigh, and he reached for it, pulled it out of the wrapping, and held it tightly. The next boat was only a few feet away. It would be easy to swing into it, as long as he was not spotted.

"You've always taken a great interest in youth, Mr.

Ambassador," Kate continued. "What are your plans now that you are president of the Youth Council?"

"All sorts of things," said Damien. "But I believe the most important task I have is to help young people gain a more prominent role in world affairs than the one we currently afford them—or rather, deny them."

Kate nodded and opened her mouth to speak, but Damien had launched into a speech.

"What is this arrogance that always makes us think we know better than they?"

Kate shook her head, but Damien was expecting no answer.

"We call them immature and naive," he continued. " 'Wait till you're grown up,' we say, 'and then we'll listen to you.' What we really mean is, 'Wait till you're grown old and then you'll think the way we do.'

"So youth stands aside, because it has no other choice, and we set to work on them."

The attention of everyone on the set was riveted on Damien. It was not often that the interviewee took such a lead so early in the proceedings or became so passionate. They listened entranced, unaware of the man crawling above them, moving from one lighting boat to another until he was poised directly above Damien. Carefully Benito raised the dagger to his lips, kissed the hilt, drew breath, summoning up his God and his courage.

"We ply them with our values," Damien continued. "We indoctrinate them with our mediocrity until finally they emerge from their brainwashing education as so-called fully fledged citizens.

"Clipped," he said precisely, gazing into the eye of the camera. "Impotent. But, above all, safe."

Benito moved into a crouch, his eyes fixed on the top of Damien's head. He rose unsteadily to his feet and leaned back to balance himself for the leap, rocking the boat, the change of weight causing it to jerk to one side, the sudden tension snapping a support chain. The boat dipped. A second chain snapped, and Benito slipped onto his knees and slithered the length of the boat, clawing for a grip and dislodging clamps.

Kate looked up and shouted a warning, but Damien had already dived from his seat. The boat hurtled past him, two of the arc lamps breaking loose and exploding on the floor with all the force and effect of an incendiary bomb. Behind the set, heavy nylon curtains burst into flame as if they had been soaked in gasoline.

As Benito fell, a cable twisted around his ankle, breaking his fall and swinging him upside down across the set.

He screamed, but it was a cry of rage rather than fear. As he swung back into the darkness, crashing though a plywood partition, he shrieked in frustration, and as he swung forward again toward the drapes, he thought only of how foolish he must look and how ashamed he was; how demeaning to be arrested and taken away by police. He would never be able to face Father De Carlo. He was a foolish failure. Even as he hit the drapes and the flames singed his face, he felt no panic. He would soon be cut down and led away.

His hair was the first part of him to catch, burning instantly like a clump of dry grass in a bonfire. His eyelashes and eyebrows vanished and his skin blackened.

He tried to scream, but this time there was no sound. He was choking, wondering why he could not see or breathe, unable to comprehend the fact that the

71

drapes had wrapped themselves around his face and body, clinging to him as he swung back and forth, a molten shroud, keeping the air from his body as his flesh roasted on his bones.

Damien watched as technicians ran in panic around him. Someone found an extinguisher, wrestled with it, and aimed it at the flames. As he watched, Damien was reminded of something he had read, that the heart and the brain were the last organs to cook. As he dwelled on that thought, he noticed something and darted forward, ignoring Dean's shout of warning. He bent low, snatched up the gleaming object, then ran quickly back to the door.

As he reached it, he turned back. The body reminded him of a giant chrysalis, steaming now and dripping with foam. Part of the drapes had melted, and he could see the face of the man, charred, blackened, inhuman. The feet, he noticed with satisfaction, were still kicking, and they continued to twitch spasmodically as Dean took his arm and guided him through the door.

The journey to Pereford, Damien's country house, took forty minutes, and in all that time, as the big limousine cruised westward, the two men did not exchange a word. Damien gazed through the window, and Dean, who was normally talkative and busy, stared sightlessly at his newspaper, his face pale with shock. It was not until they were in Damien's study and Dean had the gin bottle in his hand that the silence was broken.

"Boy, do I need a drink," Dean muttered. "I keep seeing that horrible face." He looked over his shoulder as Damien came in behind him. "You want one?"

Damien shook his head, laid his coat on a chair, and held the dagger up to the light.

"It was an assassination attempt," he said quietly.

Dean turned and gazed wide-eyed at Damien.

"Sit down."

He did as he was told, sipping gin as Damien taught him a history lesson, of the men named Bugenhagen who had fought Satan for centuries. Nine hundred years earlier, Bugenhagen had destroyed a son of Satan; then again, in 1710, another Bugenhagen had arisen to attack the Devil Child and prevent his sacred destiny from being fulfilled; the Bugenhagens, the watchdogs of Christ. . . .

Dean reached for the bottle.

"You have heard of Megiddo?" Damien asked.

Dean shook his head.

"The underground town of Megiddo near Jerusalem, once called Armageddon. Bugenhagen lived there only twenty years ago. It was he who discovered the daggers." Damien held the dagger to the light and gazed at it. "It was Bugenhagen who gave them to my father. Seven daggers. Robert Thorn tried to destroy me. I last saw this dagger when I was six years old, raised like this in Thorn's hand." He stretched upward and the blade glinted, reflecting the firelight. "He tried to kill me, but I was protected by my own true father."

For a moment he stood like a statue, the dagger poised to strike, then he lowered it and slumped into a chair.

Dean gulped from his glass, then blew bad air from his lungs.

"You say there are seven of these," he said. "So where are the other six?"

"That," said Damien, "is what we are going to find

73

out. They must have been dug up from the museum in Chicago."

Dean looked up, his face a study of bewilderment. "There was a fire," Damien continued. "You must remember." Dean nodded. "Everything was destroyed," Damien said quietly. "Nothing was saved. Not even my aunt and uncle."

"Your uncle was killed?" Dean said.

"A boiler exploded. They were buried in the basement. No one knew at the time that they had gone to the museum."

"But how do you . . . ?" Dean caught Damien's expression and stuttered to a halt. It was an expression he had seen before, of amusement tinged with contempt. Of course Damien would know. No one else would know, but Damien would know. Nothing escaped him.

"The only things to survive, it seems," Damien continued, "were the daggers, and now they have found their way into the hands of someone who knows who I am."

"And whoever knows who you are," Dean murmured, "must also know the prophecy."

"That the birth of the Nazarene is imminent." Damien gazed at the Christ on the hilt of the dagger, then looked up at Dean. "Get on to Buher right away. Tell him to get to Chicago as soon as he can. Tell him—"

He was interrupted by a knock on the door. It opened, and Damien's butler looked in.

"Excuse me, sir," he said, "but the Harley Street Hospital has just telephoned for Mr. Dean."

"Barbara," said Dean, slapping his forehead, a cloud of guilt crossing his face. "She went into labor this afternoon." He turned to Damien. "Do you mind if . . . ?"

"Sure," said Damien. "Take the car, but call Buher first, from the embassy."

"But Buher's in Washington," Dean said, "tied up with the Israeli operation. Schroeder is dropping the Aswan Dam bombshell tomorrow at four a.m., and Buher's got to be at the White House to—"

Damien glanced at him. "You idiot, haven't you understood? They're out to destroy *me* . . . and if they destroy me, everyone goes down with me. And I mean *everyone*."

Dean turned and left the room, leaving Damien alone with the dagger. He moved to the window and gazed at the sky, his lips moving in an almost inaudible whisper:

"And what rough beast, its hour come round at last, slouches towards Bethlehem to be born?"

Father De Carlo and the five monks, clustered around the table in Cable Street, gazed dumbly at the flickering screen of the old television. When the news report was over, Father De Carlo crossed himself and rose to his feet, gazed out of the window, and turned back, trying to assimilate the news. He thought back to his first meeting with Benito, when the monk was a novice. He had been a dutiful student, quiet and dedicated, fighting as a youth to overcome an unruly, worldly streak. But he had succeeded and had given his life to God. And now God had taken it. But it was such a terrible way to die.

" 'An unidentified intruder,' " Paolo repeated, quoting the news.

Father De Carlo turned, trying to recall the exact

wording of the story. "There was no mention of the dagger, was there?" he asked.

"No," said Paolo. "They seem to be treating it as an accident."

"Thorn knows it was no accident," said Father De Carlo softly, as if to himself.

"No." Again it was Paolo, the stubborn one, the one with the photographic memory and the eye for detail. "The statement from the American Embassy said Thorn was satisfied that there was no connection between him and what he called the 'unfortunate victim.'"

Father De Carlo looked at the big man and smiled affectionately. Paolo was so precise, so pedantic. Everything was black and white to him, cut and dried. The news had said that there was no connection, and so to Paolo there *was* no connection: so gullible, so naive. They were all so naive.

Thorn knew, all right. Now he had been forewarned and would be on his guard. The death of Benito had made the job twice as difficult for the rest of them. But there was no point arguing with Paolo. Let them believe what they wished. It was not important. He could not allow them to wallow in despair.

He moved to the table and called for silence.

"Our priority now is to locate the Holy Child as soon as He is born," he said. "Brother Simeon and Brother Antonio, I want you to make ready to come with me tonight to ascertain His birthplace, for the hour draws near."

Two monks nodded, looking up at him devotedly, glad to be included.

"The rest of you must wait till we return before we decide how to proceed. Our efforts must be strictly coordinated next time. We cannot afford a second mistake."

Chairs scraped against the cracked linoleum as the monks stood up, murmuring to themselves, stoking up their courage for the conflict to come.

8

A tingling in his fingers caused Damien to blink. He had been gazing at the sky for so long he had lost all track of time. He looked down at his hands, where he had been gripping the dagger. The knuckles were white, the fingers turning blue. He dropped the dagger and began rubbing his hands together, catching sight of his watch, the one given to him by the President; it was a garish piece of equipment, the epitome of bad taste, but he forced himself to wear it as a gesture of diplomacy. On the dial, figures and digits raced around the face chasing one another. You could tell the time, the date, the temperature, humidity, God knows what, the President had said.

It was shockproof, waterproof, magnetized, hurricane-proof, lightning-proof . . . you could climb Everest with it, cross the Sahara with it, the President had claimed jocularly. You could even go down a thousand fathoms and it would still keep perfect time.

Damien had thanked him, wondering when he would ever need to know the time at the bottom of the ocean.

It was ten thirty-five on March 23. He whistled under his breath, realizing that he had been standing at this window in the study for almost half an hour, lost in thought. He glanced once more at the sky, feeling the blood flow back into his fingers, then turned and left the room, making his way up the wide staircase to the first floor.

"George."

A door opened, and the butler looked out.

"I won't be needing anything else tonight."

"Very good, sir. Goodnight."

Damien stood and waited till the man had closed the door, thinking back to the drama of the evening, and the dead man, hanging from a chain. He glanced at his palm, seeing the impression still left by the dagger, and instantly he was filled with a cold rage.

He made his way along the gallery which overlooked the entrance hall. Running his fingers along the rail, he glanced downstairs, a flash of memory jolting him. He was a boy, just a child on a toy bicycle. His mother balanced on a stool, reaching upward with a pitcher toward the plants. He remembered pedaling the toy around and around in circles, making noises with his lips; vroom, vroom, closer and closer to his mother, feeling mischievous. He remembered the look of concern on her face, her mouth opening, telling him to be careful, the concern turning to panic as he pedaled faster in a straight line, hitting the stool, sending her backward over the railing screaming onto the tiled floor. He remembered the fear and shock he had felt and the strange exhilaration, as if he had done something wonderful. . . .

He moved on out of the light into a dark corridor, his pupils adjusting accordingly, walking quickly and purposefully. He turned a corner, moved down a second corridor and then a third. As he passed an open door, the dog moved out of the room and padded behind him, panting heavily, the eyes dull and yellow in the blackness.

Finally he stopped at the end of a narrow corridor. He bent and unlocked the door, slipped inside, and closed it. The dog settled itself outside, staring back the way it had come, its tongue out, flexing to the rhythm of its breath.

The room was a black chapel. It was circular, the roof supported by six columns. It was empty except for a cross which stood in the middle of the room and dominated it. Nailed to it was a life-sized figure of Christ, the body wrapped around it in a perverse interpretation of the Crucifixion. The face and chest were pressed against the upright, the legs were wrapped around it, the arms were stretched out along the beam and nailed through the back of the hands. He was naked.

A single shaft of light sliced down from the ceiling onto the Christ figure, emphasizing the emaciated body, the ribcage, and the knobs of the spine.

On the far wall, the face of a child stared back at him, a beautiful boy, painted by a madman, a man who claimed to have been visited by Satan and who spent his life creating visions of him. He had painted the child countless times, once on a wall which had survived the centuries and been discovered by the archaeologist Bugenhagen. All those who had seen the wall had died, for it was the face of Damien Thorn as a child. Damien looked at a vision of his past, then turned and stared into the gloom.

"O my father," he prayed softly. "Lord of Silence, Supreme God of Desolation, whom mankind reviles yet aches to embrace, strengthen my purpose to save the world from a second ordeal of Jesus Christ and his grubby, mundane creed."

He paused. "Two thousand years have been enough."

He moved forward and stood gazing at the cross.

"Show man instead the rapture of *thy* kingdom," Damien continued. "Infuse in him the grandeur of melancholy, the divinity of loneliness, the purity of evil, the paradise of pain."

He cursed in exasperation. "What perverted imagination has fed mankind the lie that Hell festers in the bowels of the earth?

"There is only one Hell—the leaden monotony of human existence. There is only one Heaven—the ecstasy of my father's kingdom."

He raised his hands, palms outward, and stared at the back of Christ's head. In the gloom of the chapel, his eyes gleamed yellow.

"Nazarene charlatan," he roared. "What can *you* offer humanity?"

He paused, almost as if expecting an answer, then continued his diatribe.

"Since the hour you vomited forth from the gaping wound of a woman, you have done nothing but crush man's soaring desires in a deluge of sanctimonious morality."

He stepped forward, his face only a few inches from Christ's neck, then grasped the cross as if trying to crush the twisted body. Spitting saliva, he snarled into the ear of the image.

"You have inflamed the pubertal mind of youth with your repellent dogma of original sin, and you are resolved to deny him ultimate joy beyond death by destroying me. But you will fail, Nazarene, as you have always failed."

The violence of his words seemed to exhaust him, and he bowed his head, his hair on Christ's shoulder, his hands holding the body in a brutal caress. When he raised his head again, his voice was more controlled.

"We were both created in man's image, but while you were born of an impotent God, I was conceived of a jackal, born of Satan, the Desolate One, the Nail." He shook his head, a forelock whipping across Christ's shoulders. "Your pain on the cross was but a splinter compared to the agony of my father, cast out from heaven, the Fallen Angel. Banished. Reviled."

He reached out and grasped the head of Christ, the crown of thorns digging into his palms.

"I would drive deeper the thorns into your rancid carcass, you profaner of vices, accursed Nazarene."

He leaned back, closed his eyes, and roared, his voice broken, a howl of anguish: "O Satan, beloved father, I will avenge thy torment by destroying the Christ forever."

He screamed as the metal cross of thorns gouged their way into his palms.

Blood trickled slowly from his hands into the eyes of Christ and flowed, as red tears, down the Messiah's stricken face.

9

Twenty miles to the south, John Favell drove through the Downs, stoking up his curiosity and feeding his excitement. He had checked the weather forecast, praying, praying to a God he no longer acknowledged, that there would be no clouds, and his prayers had been answered. He would be able to record the alignment, the Trinity alignment as he had named it. Not the Holy Trinity or any mumbo-jumbo—there was no need to complicate matters by bringing in religious adjectives; no need whatsoever.

Then there was the priest. At first, when the man had written, asking permission to visit, Favell had muttered angrily that the whole thing was getting out of hand, that he should never have informed him in the first place. A simple act of courtesy had resulted in his routine being broken, for he never allowed anyone inside the observatory. Visitors asked silly questions and got in the way. But as he thought about it, his curiosity grew. There was no harm in it, and it would be interesting to see the reaction of someone nonscientific; he would be like an anthropologist viewing the primitives.

He turned a corner, and as he gazed up at the vast receiving dish of the observatory, silhouetted against the night sky, he remembered the words of a friend. The man had surprised him by saying that after fifteen years of marriage, he was still thrilled by the sight of his wife undressing for bed. John Favell felt the same about his work.

He rode the elevator and stepped into the neon glare of the observation area. Barry, his technician, was already at work, and they exchanged their usual greetings.

For the first few hours the two men busied themselves with routine tasks, but neither could concentrate. They were checking their watches when the door buzzer rasped. Barry crossed the room and picked up the answerphone, listened, and turned to Favell.

"It's the mad monk," he said.

"Don't blaspheme," said Favell, smiling. "Just let him in."

"Them," said Barry, pressing a button and unlocking the door downstairs.

"What?"

"There are three of them."

"Damn," said Favell. There was hardly room for them. He swore again. They're probably bringing gold, frankincense, and myrrh, he thought, and tutted like a spinster.

But as Father De Carlo entered, with Simeon and Antonio behind him, his irritation disappeared. They seemed so gentle, so humble and dignified, just as monks should be.

Father De Carlo made the introductions.

"We all thank you for telling us about the Trinity," he said.

"There's no need," said Favell brusquely, feeling embarrassed.

"God will reward you," said Father De Carlo.

"I'm afraid I don't subscribe to your . . ."

"He will reward you anyway," said Father De Carlo simply.

Favell shrugged and showed them around, telling them that the telescope was the finest of its kind in the world. He showed them the computer, the data panels, and the monitors, spread some of his transparencies on the light box, illustrating the movement of the three suns. He was talking so much he scarcely heard their question.

"We are interested to know where the birth will take place," said Father De Carlo.

"We shall be able to define the spot of maximum intensity to within the nearest square meter."

He turned back to the telescope and saw Barry looking pointedly at his watch. Nodding, he ushered the three men to the far side of the room, placing them, like guests at a dinner party, around the scanning monitor.

They looked up at a starfield glistening with a myriad of suns and planets.

"Just keep watching," said Favell. "We shall do the rest."

"And the numbers?" asked Father De Carlo, pointing to the two sets of digits in the top right-hand corner.

"Days, hours, minutes," said Favell. "The fast one is a countdown of seconds."

He left them staring up at the screen, the youngest one open-mouthed, and returned to the console. It was a complex piece of equipment, and Barry had once compared it to a starship bridge, saying that one day he was going to take the observatory to Mars. But now not even Barry was in the mood for levity. Favell looked over at him by the controls, then turned his attention to the two monitors before him. One showed the starfield. The other was a grid map of the western hemisphere. He glanced at the digits in the corner, flexed his fingers, and bent toward the intercom, his earlier excitement forgotten, all his energy and attention concentrated on the screen before him.

"Convert to X ray eighty-four," he said.

He leaned back, adjusted the monitor slightly, and bent forward again.

"Select declination at forty-four degrees twenty-one, framing on the AR-4 precinct."

The telescope focused on the area, zooming through the starfield so quickly that Father De Carlo felt dizzy.

"Hold."

The picture on the monitor was still.

"Super polarizing filter one A."

The screen darkened, and Favell checked the time sequence. From the three men came a sigh of wonder as they saw the sky in sharp focus above them, but Favell did not hear them. He was at one now with his machine, an armchair space voyager. Had the observatory been on fire, he would scarcely have noticed.

For a few seconds the screen remained static. Then, from the bottom two corners and the top center, a glow seeped onto the screen. Father De Carlo caught his breath, his hands automatically coming together, fingers touching, in a gesture of prayer.

Gradually the three areas of light moved toward one another, steadily brightening until the screen flared. The light was unbearable, and Antonio backed off, his hands over his eyes.

"Super polarizing filter ten," Favell said sharply.

The filter cut across the screen, dimming the glare as the three suns converged; molten shimmering discs. Father De Carlo blinked, thinking he could distinguish great tongues of fire leaping across from their surfaces. He glanced across to Favell, wanting to talk to him, to listen to what he had to say, to have some sort of commentary, but the man was absorbed in his work, his eyes flitting from the suns to the digital readout and onto the grid map which showed three rings converging on one another.

Favell barked instructions once more, and the map changed, moved into closeup, showing the alignment of the suns, their point of maximum intensity, indicating that the glare would be the greatest over the British Isles.

De Carlo glanced at the seconds snapping away in the corner:

0012
0011
0010
009
008
007

He made the sign of the Cross and held his breath.

Favell's eyes were dancing now, flickering from the monitor to the map, his fingers drumming on the console; and now the observatory itself began to shimmer with the reflected light from the two monitors, the three churchmen, bathed in a glow from the depths of the universe. But none of them so much as blinked.

003
002
001
000

On the monitors the screens blazed with the light, and on the map the three rings pulsated over the south of England. As one, the three churchmen dropped to their knees in prayer, and Father De Carlo wept unashamedly.

Twenty miles to the north, Damien sat up in bed, jerking upright as if he had been tugged by wires. For half an hour he had twisted and turned, thrashed around in his nightmare, and now it had become a reality. His body, the sheets, even the mattress were wet with his sweat. His eyes were bright, his mouth open in a silent scream. His fingers dug into his thighs through the sheet, and he gazed at the ceiling, seeing nothing, hearing nothing, not even aware of the howling of the dog, a dreadful wail as if its soul were being torn from its black body.

PART TWO

10

The group of demonstrators in Grosvenor Square had grown steadily throughout the morning until by lunchtime there was a big enough crowd to warrant bringing in extra police from the Snow Hill Station. Reporters arrived, followed by television crews, and as soon as the cameras were set up, the crowd grew even larger, and their chants could be heard in Oxford Street and Park Lane.

As the Ambassador's limousine drew up, a section of the crowd tried to surge forward but were held back by a police cordon. Damien stepped out and turned to face them, looking from one banner to another.

"Condemn Israeli mass murderers."

"Where's your voice, America?"

"End your support for Jewish bastards."

His face expressionless behind the dark glasses, he

turned and made his way up the embassy steps through a crowd of reporters.

"How do you feel, Mr. Ambassador?" asked one, as they clustered round him.

"Never felt better."

"Do you think there's any connection between the accident at BBC and today's news?"

"None whatever," he said sharply.

He reached the door, the reporters and the television crews behind him jostling for position. One voice rang out clearly above the others.

"What's your comment on Schroeder's revelation that the Israelis were responsible for the Aswan Dam disaster?"

"If it's true," said Damien, turning to face them, "then it's a bitter blow to world peace."

"Is that an official condemnation?" asked another voice.

"I condemn all violence," said Damien. "But it is too early to be specific."

"The Soviet Union has offered its full support to Egypt. How do you react to that?"

Damien held up his hands in apology as one of his security men opened the door.

"I'm sorry, gentlemen, but I have no further comment to make at this time."

He was making his way into the building when he heard his name being called. He turned and saw Kate trying to claw her way toward him.

"Good morning, Miss Reynolds." He nodded to the security man and stood back to let her squeeze past him into the embassy, leaving the reporters grumbling among themselves about bloody women, bloody television, unfair advantages, and other inferences which were none too polite.

Kate walked with Damien toward the elevators, and she tried to catch her breath.

"I tried calling you last night," she said, "but there was no reply." She looked up at him, still embarrassed by the tragedy at the studio. "Isn't there anything we can do to make up for it?"

"Like what, for instance?" Damien stopped at the elevator and pressed a button.

Kate shrugged. She could do nothing but apologize. As she scrabbled round in her mind for something to say, Damien came to her rescue.

"Like finishing your interview, perhaps?"

She nodded, grateful to him.

"But I'd sooner you did it at my place," he continued. "Yours is a little too dramatic for my taste."

Kate nodded, feeling relieved. Behind Damien the elevator doors opened. He took off his glasses and held the door open. "You could stay on to dinner afterward, if you like." He stepped into the elevator. "Just the three of us."

Kate blinked in confusion.

"You, me, and Peter," he said.

Peter? she thought. Why Peter? And the words tumbled out fast before she had time to stop herself. "Well, thank you, but don't feel that Peter has to come too."

"I'd like him to," he said. And as the elevator closed, he smiled at her.

Kate turned away, angry at herself. Why had she blurted out these words? It was almost as if she were throwing herself at him. "Oh no, not Peter," she muttered, mimicking herself. "Just the two of us for dinner. Never mind the boy." She realized with a sudden flash of self-awareness that she was actually jealous of her own son, jealous of the easy way he got on with

Damien, as if the boy and the man shared some secret, as if they were talking about her behind her back. It was ridiculous. She swore under her breath, aware that one of the security men was watching her, probably wondering who this crazy broad was, marching through the embassy, cursing and frowning.

She smiled at him as she reached the door. Next time she would be more ladylike. If Damien was such a gentleman, then she would act accordingly. Bring your son, he was saying, so that no one will jump to conclusions. Such a diplomat. As she left the building, she wondered idly what this perfect gentleman had been doing the night before, for, by the look of his eyes, he had not slept a wink.

The leather and mahogany of former Ambassador Andrew Doyle's day had given way to Regency furniture. Harvey Dean, standing at the window, the telephone at his ear, felt a sense of *déjà vu*, as if he were back in Chicago gazing down at a riot. He could see the demonstrators clearly. Even through the double glazing and soundproofing, he could faintly hear their chants, and as he spoke he was counting heads, trying to calculate the size of the crowd.

"What time did the White House get it?" he said into the receiver.

He nodded at the answer and glanced at his watch. "So it's two-thirty our time. I guess we should get a response by . . . what? Noon, your time?"

He paused, seeing a wedge of police move in from the right-hand corner of the square.

"I haven't seen anything like it since the gas riots," he said, and there was a trace of smug satisfaction in his voice. "I just hate to think what it's like down at the Israeli Embassy."

He turned away and moved into the middle of the room, trailing the telephone wire behind him, his expression changing to a triumphant grin.

"No," he said, "a boy. My wife has given me a son. And naturally he's a beautiful child."

He accepted the congratulations being given on the phone and looked up as Damien entered the room.

"See you later, Paul," he said and hung up.

Damien's official smile had vanished. Now that the office doors were closed behind him, he could give himself over to his mood, which was ugly.

"That was Buher," said Dean brightly, unaware of the change in atmosphere, the depression that had settled on the office. "He's just sent the NLF report to the White House. He says it's so full of holes you could drive a truck through it."

Damien walked silently across to the window, saying nothing.

"Thanks for the flowers," Dean said. "Barbara really appreciated them."

"And the daggers?" The words were spat at him, the tone irritable. This was no time to talk of flowers.

Dean looked up, his head cocked to one side, his eyes bright through his spectacles, his joviality gone.

"Buher's got the disciples working on that," he said, trying to sound businesslike. "Apparently they came up for auction and were bought recently by a priest who passed them on to a monastery in Italy." He moved to the desk and glanced at his notes.

"Subi . . . something or other." He squinted.

"Subiaco," said Damien. "The Monastery of San Benedetto."

"That's it," said Dean, nodding in agreement, glad that Damien had said something. It wasn't much but it was something. Encouraged, he continued, "We've got our Italian people working on it, so—"

"Too late," said Damien sharply. "The birds will have flown."

He continued staring out the window, talking to himself as if Dean did not exist. "They're in England for the birth of the Nazarene, trying to destroy me before I can destroy them."

He gazed at the sky.

"He was born last night."

Dean blinked and leaned back against the desk, his notes fluttering to the floor, dead forgotten leaves.

"I felt his presence from the moment of his birth," said Damien, turning now, acknowledging the other man's presence. "Like a virus, a parasite, feeding on my energy, trying to drain me of power "

Dean could see what he meant. For the first time he noticed how exhausted Damien looked. There were shadows under his eyes, lines etched into his face He was no longer fresh and boyish. It was as if he had grown old overnight.

"Every day that he lives and grows," Damien said in a monotone, "my force will weaken."

Again he turned away from Dean, gazing out, seeing nothing. "Are you such a coward, Nazarene, that you can't face me alone?" he said wearily. "Hide if you must, but I will hunt you down, and as you have nailed mankind to your cross of piety, so I will nail you to a cross of oblivion."

Dean shivered and moved to the window, looking down, trying to see what Damien saw, struggling to understand him and to share his pain.

He gazed at the crowd beneath him, looking from the left to right, focusing suddenly on a figure in the center of the demonstration. He frowned, startled, turned, and called out to Damien, who followed the direction of his pointed finger.

Among the placards held high and prominently:

REJOICE FOR CHRIST IS REBORN

And the two men stared down into the eyes of a man in the dress of a lay preacher, a man who returned their gaze, staring up at them, unblinking, with the expression of triumph.

Damien flinched and sprang back as if he had been punched. Wearily he shook his head and slumped into his chair.

With the coming of nightfall, the demonstration had died out, bedraggled groups of protesters dispersing and leaving the square deserted except for one man, sitting on a bench, feeding pigeons, his banner lying beside him.

Every few minutes, Brother Matteus looked up at the building, seeing the lights go out and checking the staff as they left by the various exits. Once when a limousine eased its way to the front he stood up and padded across the grass, but no one came near it and the driver settled himself in his seat, his cap over his eyes, dozing.

Eventually only a single light shone. Matteus stared at the two men in the window.

"Rejoice," he said softly, "for Christ is reborn."

In the embassy, Dean had become restive. The afternoon had been wasted. Work had piled up but Damien had refused to attend to it; instead, he stared moodily into the square, saying nothing. It had gotten so bad that Dean had made unnecessary trips to the washroom; anything to get away from that terrible gloom.

He looked up at Damien and grunted down at the square. The man had not moved.

"What's he doing, just sitting there?" he said irritably.

"Waiting for me," Damien answered in a monotone. "To follow him into a trap."

Dean snorted in disgust. "He must be an idiot." He felt like shaking his fist at the man, calling out the cops to move him on. His very presence was an insult. "What makes him think you're going to fall for something like that?"

"Because he knows that's exactly what I intend to do."

Dean shrugged his shoulders. It made no sense to him. None of it. He remembered the man at the studios, the burned corpse, and a thought occurred to him.

"But what if he's got one of the daggers?"

Damien went to the desk, picked up a pair of binoculars, and trained them on Matteus.

"I'll be wasting my time if he hasn't," he said.

Dean shook his head. It was all too much for him. None of it made sense. Damien was talking in riddles again. But perhaps it was just as well. Maybe it was better not to know.

11

From the window of the train, Brother Matteus watched the figure of Father De Carlo recede into a small speck by the barrier. He waved one last time, then made his way to his seat. When he sat down he glanced at his watch. It was not yet midday, but already he was exhausted. He had had a terrible night, tossing and turning, the nightmare and the moments of awakening merging into one another. He could not remember which one of his brothers had kept awakening him, asking if he was all right. It was Simeon, he thought, or maybe Martin. And which one in the nightmare kept beckoning to him? Which was the monk with the body of a man and the face of a beast?

He shivered. Not since he was a young man, when the forces of good and evil were fighting for possession of his soul, had he suffered such torture.

When at last he had drifted into a dead sleep, the others had allowed him to lie on his cot. He awakened in a panic, but Father De Carlo had calmed him. The others had gone ahead, the priest had said. Now it was his turn.

He looked out at the urban sprawl of West London but saw nothing. For thirty years he had been at peace with his God and with himself. There were no doubts and no fears. Until last night.

He remembered as a young man being cursed with desires of the flesh. The Devil had tempted him with doubts and had shown him forbidden pleasures. It had been a struggle before he finally came down on the right side of the fence and walked in the presence of the Lord. He remembered Benito telling him the same thing, only with Benito, the struggle had been much more recent. And now Benito was at one with God. . . . Matteus bowed his head in prayer and asked for strength.

When he looked up again he realized that this was the first time he had been alone since he had entered the monastery. In Subiaco he was never alone, and the few times he went out to the village he went with others.

He glanced at his fellow passengers. The man seated next to him was busy with the contents of a briefcase. A family on the opposite side of the aisle was eating lunch, peeling wrappers from sandwiches and pouring tea from a thermos flask. Ahead sat two women. They were so brazen, these women, exposing their flesh in their tight, brief garments.

He clutched the shoulder bag close. He would not put it on the rack or under his seat lest someone pick it up in error. Through the lining he could feel the outline of the dagger, and he began to perspire. Would he be able to use it when the time came? Would he be able to bury it to the hilt in bone and flesh? Could he bear the screams? The flash of his nightmare returned, and he gazed through the window. It was not safe to daydream. When he lost concentration, the terrors returned. He contented himself with gazing around the carriage, avoiding the sight of the two women.

"Let it be me, Father," he had pleaded on Sunday. "Let me be the one." But it was Benito who had gone, and now it was his turn. An idea sneaked uninvited into his brain. Why had he been so insistent? If he had not made such a fuss, then perhaps he would have been waiting back at Cable Street for news of the others. He frowned and scolded himself. What he was doing was an honor and a privilege. He recalled his first glimpse of the Anti-Christ and the thrill of recognition, remembering the way he had forced himself to speak the words of the Lord as if the saying of them would protect him; yet those eyes seemed to drill through to the back of his skull, yellow, mad, animal eyes; but he had held Damien Thorn's gaze.

"He would have read your thoughts as surely as you read his," the priest had said. And it was these words which had put the idea into his head. The Anti-Christ would follow him. He would stalk to find the Christ Child. Matteus had quite deliberately put himself up as bait, and the role both excited and scared him.

Maybe Thorn would be on the train, he thought, traveling first-class. But no. He had his own transportation—helicopters, all manner of things. It would be no problem for Damien to follow him; on that fact, Matteus and the others were pinning their faith.

He reached into his bag for one of the books he had brought from Italy, but he could not concentrate on the text. He gazed at the countryside as the train sped through Reading and on to Oxford, and by the time it reached the university town he was drowsy, lulled to sleep by the motion and the fetid air. And it was then that the scavengers returned to haunt him.

He awoke with his mouth open, gurgling like a baby, a man in uniform bending over him, asking him if he was all right. Passengers were on their feet. He nodded and apologized, and they went back to their seats.

From then on, all the way to his destination, he kept his eyes open, aware that people were continuing to stare curiously at him.

It was late afternoon when he got off the train, climbed a bridge to another platform, and boarded a smaller train, an old machine with small compartments and no corridor. He looked behind him. No one had gotten off the express. He settled back, alone in the carriage, with the smell of horsehair strong in his nostrils.

The second stage of the journey was made in silence. Apart from the clatter of the engine and the squeak of the carriage, there was nothing. The countryside was green and featureless and the small stations empty. The train stopped repeatedly, but from his position Matteus never saw anyone enter or leave. He gazed at the old photographs on the wall of the compartment, faded pictures of British beauty spots. He took out the dagger and played with it. Again he tried to read but could not concentrate, and it was with some relief that he reached his destination.

As he stepped out onto the platform, one of his legs buckled, stiff from sitting so long, and he almost tumbled. It was dusk now and he could see no one. He stared up and down the platform and watched the train rattle away around a bend and out of sight.

There was no one to take his ticket, and so he left it by the barrier and stepped out into a country lane. Clutching his shoulder bag, he walked across to a bus stop and waited.

Bait . . . The word crept into his imagination. He thought of worms twisting on fishing hooks, goats tethered waiting for the tiger, bloody chum spread on the ocean to attract sharks. He shuddered and forced himself to think of other things.

He looked all around him, but the only movement was on the skyline, crows wheeling and cawing among the trees. He kicked at a clump of grass and wandered up and down the road. When the bus finally turned the corner, he sighed with relief.

There were two men seated up front near the driver. He nodded to them and made his way along the aisle to the back. As the bus moved off, he saw a Range Rover drive out of a lane half a mile away and turn into the road. He gazed at it as it came closer and recognized the face of the driver. For a moment the two men gazed at one another until the Range Rover slowed and dropped behind, following the bus at a distance of about two hundred yards.

Matteus sat down, aware that his whole body was pulsing and his hands trembling. So, the bait had been taken.

He was struck with a strange desire. He wished that he had a son to whom he could tell this story, a child who would listen and be proud of him, but instantly he dismissed the fantasy, scolding himself for the sin of vanity.

The bus stopped twice. At the second stop the two men got out, leaving him alone again. The road was a single track now. There were no longer any farm-houses or inns, just moorland and sheep. The bus brushed against the verge as it drove deeper into the countryside. Every few hundred yards, the verge had been gouged away to make a passing place, but nothing approached them. The bus was the only vehicle on the road, except for the Range Rover half a mile behind.

Matteus opened the bag again and took out the small radio set Father De Carlo had given him. He touched the controls and held it to his ear. He had never seen or used a two-way radio before, a walkie-talkie they called it, but he felt glad to have it. It was good to know that through the little box he could talk to friendly voices. They would not be far away now. He checked his map and stood up.

The sound of the engine changed as the driver went through the gears. The bus turned a sharp bend and slowed down. The man turned and told him this was the last stop before the long trail to the coast. Matteus thanked him and clambered out, feeling as though he had been traveling for days. The bus drove off out of sight, and Matteus waited for the Range Rover to appear, but there was nothing, neither sight nor sound of it.

He looked for the twentieth time at his map, grunted in satisfaction when he saw the stile and the track across the moors. He climbed it, feeling stiff and glad to be walking, to get the feeling back in his legs. He took deep breaths, filling his lungs and commanding himself not to look behind him or talk to the placid sheep which munched on the grass and looked blankly toward him.

He had gone only a few yards when he heard the drone of the Range Rover behind him. He turned and saw it half a mile away on the horizon, silhouetted against the dying sun.

"Good," he said aloud and strode off across the moor, glad to be out in the open, away from the claustrophobic confinement of buses and trains.

It took him twenty minutes to reach the valley. Looking up, he could make out the shape of the chapel ahead of him on an outcrop of rock. The roof had long since vanished, and the chapel reared black and jagged into the dusk. Matteus was reminded of the monastery back in Italy and realized with some surprise that he was suddenly homesick.

Looking down, he saw the white marker set into the ground. He stopped and reached into his bag for the radio, trying to remember which button to press. It was simplicity itself, they had said. He stabbed at a button and raised it to his lips. Feeling slightly foolish, he spoke into it, the sound of his voice startling the sheep.

"Matteus at the half-kilometer mark. Thorn is parallel about five hundred meters northwest of me. He is wearing a blue parka." He paused. "Over," he said.

He looked at the machine and blinked as the acknowledgment came through.

"Proceed as planned. Over and out."

Matteus smiled to himself. Modern science was wonderful. Martin's voice was as clear as a bell. He could have been standing a few feet away. He stuffed the radio into his bag and set off again, listening for the drone of the Range Rover, but it had stopped, and all he could hear was the sound of his own breathing.

The dog had remained stationary throughout the journey. It stood in the back of the vehicle, staring through the windshield. It had balanced itself against the rear seat, its great shoulders pressed against the leather, its head resting on the back of the seat, and it scarcely moved, even as the Range Rover bucked and swayed across the moor. When it stopped, the dog looked up expectantly, and when the door was opened, it padded out onto the moor, needing no instructions, moving soundlessly and invisible, black against the night sky, gaining on its quarry with every step.

It was almost time. Matteus reached the graveyard and looked up at the chapel, towering above him. He could see the moon through the shattered windows, and he congratulated Father De Carlo on his inspiration. It was a dramatic place to do the deed, in God's house; desecrated and ruined it might be, but it was God's house nonetheless. He felt satisfied. He had done his part. Now it was up to them.

Carefully he weaved his way between the tombstones. Some had collapsed, others lay slanted at an angle, leaning against their neighbors. He casually glanced at them, the inscriptions, trying to distinguish the epitaphs, but the stones were weatherbeaten and ancient, most of the words long since erased. Shadows moved among them, one bleating a warning as Matteus approached. A large ewe gazed at him, its eyes wide, and then ran, skidding on the grass, its hooves clattering on a fallen stone.

Matteus turned to watch it, smiled at its irrational fear, and when he turned back he gazed into his nightmare, into a vision of the very jaws of hell. . . .

All afternoon the two men had kept watch, building their courage by talking to one another about insignificant things as if by discussing normality they could keep the abnormal at bay.

Brother Martin had lost count of the number of

times Brother Paolo had said that Matteus was the bravest of them all, acting as bait, leading the Anti-Christ into the trap. The first time, Martin had agreed, but eventually he grew tired of the repetition and told Paolo to be quiet. He was on watch when the radio barked at him. He thanked God for Matteus' safe delivery and called Paolo to the edge of the rock.

Together they stared out into the night, but they couldn't see anything, and could hear only the bleating of a sheep and the scrabbling of hooves. The moon passed behind a cloud and reappeared, but still they saw nothing.

"He should be here by now," Paolo whispered. Even as he spoke, Martin ducked down behind the wall. He had seen him, the blue parka as Matteus had said. Grabbing Paolo's hand, Martin crept back through the broken doorway into the chapel. They moved to the massive stone altar which dominated the place and shrank back into the shadows.

Through the roof they could see the stars. Each man offered up a silent prayer and reached for his dagger. Martin looked at Paolo and nodded, then stood rigid, scarcely breathing in case the sound warned him.

They heard movement outside. He would be exhausted by the time he got to the top. It was a long climb, forty feet. Paolo remembered how his arms had ached by the time he had reached the top rung of the rusty iron ladder. And now they could hear him breathing, his breath labored, a harsh rasping in his throat. They pressed back into the cold wall and saw the figure silhouetted in the doorway.

The altar, Paolo said to himself. Go to the altar. It has to be done on the altar.

As if obeying instructions, the figure walked stiffly

forward, placed his hands on the altar, and gazed ahead, motionless, his back to the two monks.

Paolo was the first to leap, his sandaled feet slapping against the flagstones, the dagger in his right hand held low. He reached for the neck, grabbed it with his left hand, and drove the dagger as he had been taught, hearing the grating of bone as the blade entered, feeling the shock run up his arm to the elbow. He wanted to leave the dagger and run, but he forced himself to push harder until he felt the smooth surface of the parka. The blade was lodged in the ribcage, driven to the hilt. Please don't scream, he murmured, but there was no sound. It was as if he had stabbed a corpse.

Now Martin was at his side, screeching something unintelligible, the dagger raised and striking downward, missing Paolo's face by inches, hitting the hood of the parka and slipping, scraping against the shoulder blade and glancing off, tearing at an angle into the spine.

Shuddering, the two men stepped back, released the daggers, and watched in horrified fascination as the body swayed upright, then slowly slumped face down on the altar. There was a soft pop as the nose broke.

For a moment there was silence, then Paolo stepped forward and made the sign of the cross.

"*In nomine Patri,*" he murmured, "*et Filii, et Spiritus Sancti* . . . Amen."

Martin, still shivering with the horror of it, moved to his side. Laboriously they turned the body over and stared into the face of Matteus, a grotesque face set in shock, the eyes sightless, rolled back in their sockets, showing only white.

Paolo and Martin jumped back, wiping their hands on their cassocks, gazing at one another, their lips moving but emitting no sound, searching for an answer where there was none.

Paolo turned away and stared at the sky, looking for something on which to focus, anything rather than that dead face.

"Sweet Savior," he said. "Spare our minds from the possession of the Anti-Christ, save us . . ."

The sound of snarling made him turn, his body whipping around. Martin had already turned and was standing motionless, silently staring into the dog's eyes. They stepped back and the dog in the doorway looked from one to the other, the jaws open, hackles raised.

The window, Paolo thought. They could climb onto the ledge and wait till the beast had gone. He felt Martin's hand tight on his arm, and he turned to the window past the altar and stared into the very sight that had driven Matteus insane.

The jackal's skull was framed in the window and gazed sightlessly back at them, the head filling the whole sky, obscuring everything, the eyes empty in their sockets, the veins pulsing rhythmically, the skull gleaming as though lit from within.

They backed away, babbling incoherently. Martin stumbled against the altar. Reaching out to balance himself, his hand grasped Matteus' hair, his fingers digging into the dead eye. He screamed and spun away, tripped again and sprawled on the flagstones. As he lay there, he saw a rusted grill on the floor, half open. Instinctively he pushed at it and gazed down. It was an old well, the walls smooth and black, cut to the base of the rock. Without hesitation he scrambled down into it, grasping the bars of the grill, his feet scrabbling for a hold, shouting for Paolo to follow. Paolo was close behind him, and together they hung in the well, fifty feet from the broken rocks below, their backs pressed against the wall, their feet searching for a grip.

They hung motionless. Paolo stared down between his knees at the sheer drop, then looked up again as he heard the padding of paws on the flagstones. The dog appeared at the edge, gazing down at them, the jaws dripping saliva on Martin's face. For a full minute it stood there as if on guard, and then the grill began to creak, sliding shut, the two men moving with it, holding on, their knuckles white, their bodies swaying away from the wall of the well, their feet dangling.

The grill clanged shut, and the dog grunted. Paolo looked at it and felt his left hand slipping, the fingers sticky with Matteus' blood. They slipped, and he swung one-handed against the wall. Briefly he hung on motionless before kicking at the wall and reaching again for the grill. At the second attempt he caught it. Paolo breathed hard and looked up. The dog stepped forward onto Martin's fingers. The monk screamed and tried to clutch the dog's leg.

"Don't move," Paolo whispered. "Leave it."

His face contorted with fear, Martin shook his head and stared into Paolo's face. His mouth opened as if to say something, his fingers slipped, and he dropped. Paolo closed his eyes, but he was unable to shut his ears to the echoing scream and the thud as Martin smashed into the rocks. And even then the screaming seemed to continue, echoing back up the well like a wail from a grave.

The dog grunted again, then stepped back out of sight. Paolo opened his eyes. He was a strong man. He knew that he could hang on for perhaps another minute and a half. It was a terribly short time to live. He cried unashamedly, the tears running down his chin. He could only hope that the pain would not last for eternity. . . .

12

It was the first warm day of the year. The spring sunshine slanted into the drawing room of Damien's country house, dazzling the television crew as they set up their equipment. Kate stood by the window gazing out across the fields. It was a magnificent place. Before she came out she had looked it up in a guidebook: Pereford; built in the seventeenth century, sixty-three rooms, two wings and a modern annex, four hundred acres of grounds.

It was all quite spectacular. She remembered Damien answering a criticism that perhaps he was being a bit ostentatious, that he did not need so many rooms for himself and his personal staff.

"My parents lived here," he had said. "I like to keep myself in the manner to which I have become accustomed."

She had wondered then if the pun had been intentional, but she doubted it. She turned and watched the

Sam Neill as Damien Thorn, head of the powerful
Thorn Corporation.

Father De Carlo (Rossano Brazzi) with the seven
deadly daggers of Meggido, instruments to destroy
the Anti-Christ.

At an Embassy party, Damien meets BBC journalist
Kate Reynolds (Lisa Harrow).

In Kensington Gardens, Damien strolls with Kate and her son, Peter (Barnaby Holm).

Kate interviews Damien on her TV program.

Damien plots a diabolical scheme with his aide, Harvey Dean (Don Gordon).

Damien begins to take possession of Peter.

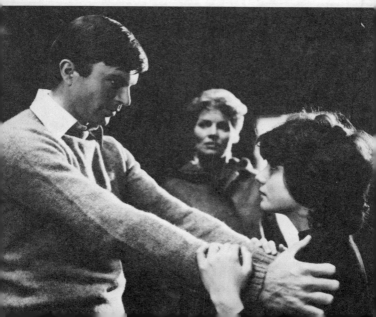

In Cornwall, Damien and Peter take part in a hunt,
ending in the violent death (below) of
Brother Antonio.

On a Cornish cliff, Damien addresses his disciples, as Dean (below) watches.

At Damien's home in Hampstead, he and Kate make violent love.

Later, Kate finds Damien lying naked on his chapel floor.

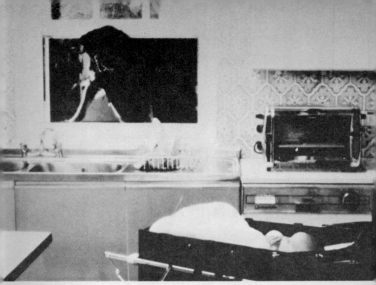

At Dean's home, a sinister dog tries to enter the window to attack his baby.

At a lonely Celtic chapel, the final conflict takes place.

crew at work. Normally a taciturn, cynical bunch, they were whistling and joking. It was remarkable what a spot of sun could do.

On the terrace, Damien and Dean looked at the spring flowers with distaste. Both men preferred autumn. They strolled in silence, Dean wondering when Damien would return to normality. The strain was spreading to the rest of the staff, and Dean himself felt affected by it, as if Damien's torture was something contagious. Dean had not been sleeping too well, and he was becoming irritable. He could also have done without that Reynolds woman always hanging about. She was part of the trouble. But then it was none of his business.

He decided to break the long brooding silence.

"So, four have been accounted for," he said.

Damien nodded. "There are three daggers left, but I can't afford to waste time any longer." He paused and continued, speaking softly, "The only way to be rid of the Nazarene is to exterminate every male child in the country born between midnight and dawn on March twenty-fourth."

At first Dean could hardly believe what he had heard. He looked at Damien, at the set expression, and he whistled, trying to take in the enormity of the suggestion.

"But how can we be sure he's still in the country?" he asked weakly.

"Their prophecy says he will come forth out of the Angel Isle," Damien said. "And one thing about these pedantic Christians, they stick to the letter of their prophecies."

They moved into the garden, walking side by side. Damien snapped a bud from a rhododendron bush and began peeling it.

"How's Barbara?" he asked.

"Fine."

"And your son?"

Dean tried to hide the shiver of apprehension, reluctant to reach the dreadful conclusion to which Damien was pointing him.

"Fine, fine," he said.

They heard a shout behind them, and Dean turned to see Peter running toward them. He had never been so glad to see anyone in his life, but Damien paid no attention to the boy, his gaze remaining fixed on Dean.

"He was born on March twenty-fourth, wasn't he?"

"Who?" Dean felt ridiculous, acting dumb, playing for time.

"Your son."

"No." It was the first time he had lied to Damien. There had never been any need, or any point. The man had access to his innermost thoughts. "No, no," he repeated. "March twenty-third. Just before midnight."

Peter joined them, saying that his mother was ready for them to come in.

"Tell her half a minute," Damien said, still looking at Dean as Peter ran back to the house. He had peeled the leaves from the bud and was crushing the remains to pulp between his fingers.

"Liquidate the Nazarene," he said softly.

Dean shrugged his shoulders in exasperation. It was simple enough to say.

"But how?" he asked irritably.

"That's what the disciples are for," said Damien simply, as if stating the obvious. "Summon them to the island on Sunday. I'm taking Kate and Peter down to

Cornwall for the hunt on Saturday, so I'll make my own way there."

He turned as Peter shouted to him, then moved toward the house, smiling back at Dean, telling him to keep his chin up.

Dean watched him go. Chin up, indeed. So very British. Stiff upper lip. He would be taking tea and scones next. Quite suddenly he felt an intense hatred for Kate Reynolds. It was all her fault. She was a bad influence. And for the first time since the weekend with Paul Buher he began to feel afraid, as if he had made a terrible mistake. A small flame of rebellion rose in him, but he quickly extinguished it and made his way to the study where the files were kept. There was nowhere for him to turn, nowhere to go. He had long ago sold his soul, and there were no refunds, no rebates. It was too late for regret.

But as he reached the desk and picked up the phone, he swore that there was one thing he would never do even if it meant an eternity of torture. . . .

Thirty miles to the east in Chancery Lane, the heart of the English legal profession, a young barrister named Frank Hutchins picked up the phone, listened carefully, and hung up, his face pink with excitement. He called to his clerk and dismissed the man for the day. He checked his office to make sure no one had come in and that the switchboard was clear. That done, he went to his safe, unlocked it, took out a black address book, and laid it by the telephone.

How long had it been? he wondered. Three years since he was called, then a year of frustration before his first big job. It had been an honor, and he had done it well. He had started by fishing out a series in one of the Sunday tabloids: "Satanism, the Evil That They Do," it was called. He had checked them all out, and one call had led to another; it was a mammoth operation sorting out the diamonds among the dross. There were so many charlatans and poseurs, but eventually he had compiled his file.

And now the time had come. He worked all day without a break, and when he finally left the office that evening his ear was buzzing from the phone. Only then did he permit himself a small sherry in a bar, sitting alone, pleased with himself, the very picture of smug complacency.

It was a simple matter for Nurse Lamont to change shifts. Her friend Sharon knew about the new man in her life and knew how important he was to her. After listening for a few moments, Sharon gave in gracefully and said that she would do a double shift for her. It was the way the world worked, she said. You scratch my back and I'll scratch yours. Next time, Sharon thought, maybe she'd have a man to go away with for a weekend. Nurse Lamont thanked her, packed a weekend bag, left the hospital, and made for the station. Sharon would want to know all the details on Monday. She was looking forward to making up a story, fantasizing a little, just to give the poor fat girl a vicarious thrill. . . .

In Hampstead, Trevor Grant had worked out a plan. He knew his parents would never let him go away for the weekend—not at ten years old. If he disappeared, they would call the police and there would be trouble; and so he had phoned his cousin in Wembley and asked if he could stay. This would give him some time. By the time his mother realized that he was not going to turn up, he would be in Cornwall, and he would phone them, just to tell them not to worry. He would make up a good story. As he put the phone down he checked his pocket money, wondering whether he should steal the fare or ask Mr. Hutchins to help. He decided to steal the money. It would be good practice for later life. . . .

In Liverpool, the Reverend Graham Ross called a young lay preacher of his acquaintance and asked him if he would not mind taking the Sunday service for him. There had been a family bereavement, Ross said. The young man agreed readily, offering his condolences and trying to hide his excitement at the opportunity of taking complete responsibility for the service.

"Bless you," said Ross and returned to his vicarage. He would take the black robes to Cornwall, he thought, and his favorite lucky charm, the cross with the Christ figure hanging upside down, nailed through the feet. . . .

From his office at Alexander Fleming House, Dr. Horace Philmore of the Department of Health and Social Security Board telephoned his wife and told her that he had to attend an emergency delegate meeting that weekend. From the sound of her response, he knew that she did not believe him. She would probably check up, make phone calls, and when he returned there would be an almighty row. She would assume that he had gone away with Margo again. Well, let her shout and scream. He was beginning to enjoy their rows. They added spice to a rather dull marriage. . . .

Throughout the country, men and women and children packed bags, made their excuses, and checked their routes toward a common destination, each one with an appointment to keep and the will to do anything that Damien Thorn commanded.

13

Ever since the news had come through, Brother Antonio had been inconsolable. He had loved them all, especially Matteus, whom he had known for thirty years. He could not believe that they were gone. Gradually the grief turned to anger and to a passionate hatred for the man known as Damien Thorn. If he had him at his mercy, there would be no sudden stab wound. It would be a lingering death. Antonio lay in his bed and thought about cutting Thorn up into dozens of pieces, and to hell with the consequences. God would not punish him for such an act. Surely not: He would approve of it, Antonio was certain of it.

As he fanned the flames of his hatred, he realized that he was in danger of allowing his anger to spill over into places where it did not belong. He realized that he would need to watch his tongue when talking to the priest, for he had never agreed to the first two plans. It was crazy to attempt an attack in a guarded television studio. It was madness to put one of them up as bait, allowing Thorn to make his plans and counterattack.

But they had not listened to his objections. He had been overruled, and the fact that he had been proved right only added to his frustration. To Antonio, it was obvious. Thorn had to be caught off guard. He had to be attacked in the open, hunted out like the beast that he was. . . .

This time Father De Carlo had agreed, for indeed he had no choice. If only he had listened earlier. Antonio had always considered himself the most worldly among the group, the most practical. He had been a born woodsman, the son of a farmer. He loved animals, but he was not, like some of the others, sentimental about them. They were all God's creatures, but the beasts of the fields were ruled over by mankind, and if one of them had to die for a higher cause, then it was no time for weeping.

As the train rocked on the rails on its way west, he glanced at the young man sitting next to him. Brother Simeon was so young and tender. He was grunting in his sleep as if in the throes of a nightmare. Antonio touched his companion's forehead. It was damp. The poor boy, he thought; so sensitive. He—Antonio—never had nightmares. Father De Carlo had once said that it was because he had no imagination. But that was just the sort of thing the priest would naturally say.

All the way to his destination he thought about his plan, and worked on it. It would need careful preparation, split-second timing, and a certain degree of luck. The luck was something he had to hope for, but if the preparation was right, then it had every chance in the world to succeed.

From the beginning, it was easy. They found a pub in the village, and soon they were talking to the local farmers. The language was difficult. The men spoke a strange dialect, but somehow they managed, talking about sports and politics, subjects Antonio knew little about. But he was a good listener. By the end of the evening he and Simeon had made friends. That night in the guesthouse bed, with a bellyful of beer, Antonio decided that if he had not followed his vocation, he might have made something of himself in the world of business. For certainly he had a devious mind.

The next morning they walked the fields with one of the friendly farmers. The man never asked why Antonio was particularly interested in foxes, nor did he ask why he wanted a terrier and a horse. He just told him where he could get them. If the man wanted a terrier, that was his business. In these parts you did not ask questions. If a man wanted to tell you something, he would do so.

They walked for miles across open fields, through woodland and copses and across a viaduct spanning a gorge. They stopped and looked down at the river a hundred feet below, but Antonio was more interested in the roof of the aqueduct at the far end. A slab of rock had cracked open, and it was possible to see down into the damp earth and to distinguish quite clearly the prints which surrounded the entrance.

For an hour the vixen had lain in her den, half asleep, ears flat, relaxed. Occasionally she snuffled and stretched, tried to turn on her side, but there was no room. Once she yawned, her back legs twitching as if she were on the run.

She sniffed danger before she heard it, sitting upright, her ears forward, the antennae of her whiskers twitching in the gloom. She got to her feet, crouching low, her head brushing the roof of the den as she heard the scrabbling and yelping above her. What light there was in the den was suddenly blocked off as something clawed at the entrance.

The terrier slithered toward her, eyes gleaming, and she leaped for it, snapping at the muzzle, connecting, shaking her head as if to kill a rat, then letting go and ducking, aiming for the throat. Her back legs slipped beneath her so that she rolled on her side, underneath the dog, then scrabbled for a hold on the wall of the den. Snapping at air, the terrier tried to find fur and flesh, but the fox was too quick. Her feet digging at the earth, she ran toward the light, moving fast. Springing like a greyhound from a trap, she leaped forward until her snout banged into something and she could go no further. In panic she tried to turn, but she could not move. There was nowhere for her to go, forward or back.

Simeon had been fast, snapping the cage door shut as the fox jumped inside. He held it tight, ignoring the terrier, who appeared at his feet covered in earth, its muzzle dripping blood, yelping in pain and frustration.

Antonio, astride a gray mare, bent down and took the cage, then raised his fist in a salute of triumph.

An hour later, outside the manor house, the hunt was almost ready to set off. The riders sipped the last of the mulled wine and handed the stirrup cups to the grooms. The breath of hounds and horses rose and mingled in the early-morning mist as the horses pawed at the gravel and the hounds bumped into one another, eager to be gone.

Kate stood at the fringe of the group, smoothing down Peter's coat. He looked so handsome, she thought, in his breeches, boots, and jacket, and she was aware that he was irritated by her attention. Men going on a hunt did not need mothers fiddling around with their clothes. She forced herself to back away and let him mingle with the others, and she fought to hide her apprehension. There had been so many stories of people falling off horses, landing on their heads. . . .

A high-pitched whinnying caused her to turn. Damien had come out of the house and was striding toward a magnificent black gelding. The horse rolled its eyes and backed off, its teeth bared. Other horses caught the smell of its fear and began to grow restless. One reared into the air, unseating its rider. Others snorted and flared their nostrils.

People were muttering around her. It was odd, they were saying. What had gotten into the horses? Normally they were a placid bunch. But within seconds a groom had calmed Damien's mount. He put his foot in the stirrup and swung himself into the saddle. Despite his outfit, he reminded Kate of a character in a Western. It was the way he sat, tight in the saddle. They rode differently, the Americans, and she had to admit that he suited the occasion. A couple of photographers swooped around him, and Kate smiled. The pictures would look good in the newspapers; the U.S. Ambassador dressed to kill. It was a natural for the tabloids.

Peter had been given a pony. He sprang into the saddle and sat smiling at Kate as she moved to his side.

"Stay close to Susan at the back," she said, nodding toward a young woman on a small mare. "Don't go showing off to Damien."

"I won't," he said with that angelic smile Kate knew so well, his tacit agreement to anything she asked. He always smiled like that to humor her and then did exactly as he pleased.

"Don't worry, Peter," the woman said, leaning across and petting the pony. "You'll still get blooded."

"What does 'blooded' mean?" He looked down at his mother, eyes wide in mock innocence.

"You know perfectly well what it means," said Kate.

"No, honestly."

"It's an old hunting custom," said Susan.

"If it's your first hunt," Kate explained patiently, "and they kill a fox, they smear its blood on your cheeks." She smiled at him. "Satisfied?"

Peter nodded and grinned at her, then turned as a horn blared.

"Take care," said Kate.

Peter looked back at her curiously as he kicked at the pony's flanks. "Why do you always worry about me?"

"Because I love you," she said to his back. "Because you're all I've got."

And then they were gone, hounds and horses at a walk moving down the drive toward the open fields.

As the hunt moved to the brow of a hill, Damien was given the position next to the master of the hunt. The two men chatted amiably to one another about the possibility of a kill. It had been a long time, the master said. The damned foxes were getting too smart.

At the top of the hill, Damien looked back, counting heads. There were twenty-five riders, including Peter at the back with Susan. The boy waved, and Damien saluted him, then turned to see the master pointing down the hill to a copse a quarter of a mile away. The old man was sniffing like a dog as he sent the hounds down the hill. They ran off at top speed, noses to the ground, working as a unit, glad to be out of the kennels.

As they worked the copse, the huntsmen waited, some patiently, others standing in the stirrups, anxious to be off. Within seconds the silence was broken. The hounds raised their heads and bayed into the wind. The master blew his horn and set off down the slope, Damien moving behind him, followed by the others. They reached the copse at a gallop, slowing to a walk as they reached the thick undergrowth. Damien, peering forward, heard a cry and a bump behind him. He turned and saw a young man flat on his back. Anxiously Damien looked for Peter, then smiled as he saw him, the pony picking its way carefully between the bushes.

Damien was the first to spot the fox. His eyes narrowed and his nostrils flared. He grunted in his throat but said nothing, waiting diplomatically for the master to catch sight of it. A few seconds later the man shouted and forced his horse forward through the copse toward the hounds and the small rust-colored beast running across the fields.

Damien swung his horse's head around and gave chase. Soon he was in the lead, crouching over the horse's neck, his lips pulled back in a snarl. Within a minute he had reached the hounds and gone past the back markers, moving in behind the leaders, who looked up at him, sniffing his scent before turning their attention to their prey.

Behind him the others marveled at his horsemanship, for they had never seen the big gelding move so fast . . . and half a mile ahead, Antonio peered through his binoculars and smiled in satisfaction.

The monk stood by a fence which split the field from woodland. He lowered his binoculars and spat on the ground. It was all going to plan. Damien had split from the rest. Antonio had counted on his being in the lead. It was essential to the plan, yet something over which he had no control. But he knew that Damien would be the fastest. If it were not a sin, he would have bet on it.

He turned, moved to the gray mare, and swung into the saddle, the butt of the shotgun on his back swinging around and smacking against the cage, strapped to the pommel. Inside, the fox snarled at him, but Antonio ignored it. He rode for a hundred yards up into the trees to the spot he had chosen. He dismounted, led his horse into the trees, and tethered it. That done, he unslung his shotgun and raised it to his shoulder.

As he squinted along the sights down the track, he licked his lips. If only it were this easy, he thought. If only it could be done with a gun.

The fox sprinted into view, and he squeezed the trigger. The fox reared up and spun backward. He fired again, knowing that no one would pay any attention to the shots. They would assume it was a farmer shooting at crows.

He ran to the fox, grabbed it by the brush, and, stumbling back the way he had come, dropped the body in the bushes. He lifted the cage from the pommel and scrambled back to the path, listening to the sounds of the hounds. They were almost upon him. Quickly he opened the cage, and the vixen raced out along the path. Antonio dropped onto his face as Damien and the leading hounds came into view and raced after it.

He scrambled back to his horse, picked up the dead fox, quickly tied a length of rope to its brush, then leaped aboard the mare and guided it back toward the track, hoping he would be in time. He reached the track seconds before the main pack of hounds. As he rode among them, back the way they had come, they reared up in confusion and turned to follow him, snapping at the dead fox trailing in the dirt. Ten yards down the track, he took a fork to the right and galloped along it, the hounds following him.

He could hear the others behind him now, the beat of the hooves and the shouts as they blindly followed him and his dead fox. It had been done. He had split them. It had worked.

Moving fast, he pulled in the fox, one-handed, until he had it by the head. The track moved out of the trees up an embankment toward a waterfall, the ground sloping sharply to one side toward a disused mill. Slipping the rope off the fox, he hurled it high in the air and watched it fall, spinning, crashing thirty feet below into the decaying machinery of the old mill. But he did not pause. There was no time for celebration or congratulation. He had to hurry to keep his appointment. . . .

Damien was crouched low over the horse's neck, crooning to it, urging it along the track. He could see the fox now, and he was surprised by its speed. The beast had stamina. It seemed to be moving faster now than it had at the start. The wood thinned out, and ahead he could see a gorge, spanned by a viaduct. The fox made for it, skidded between the two gateposts, and scampered along it.

Damien pushed the horse to further effort. Once over the viaduct there was an open field. The fox would be caught in the open where there was no cover.

As he reached the viaduct he glanced over the parapet at the river. When he looked back he saw that the fox had skidded to a stop, then vanished into its den.

Damien cursed and reined in the horse, the hounds speeding past him, scrabbling at the mouth of the den and howling in frustration.

He dismounted, breathing heavily, took off his hat, and wiped his brow. The master had been right. This looked like another day of failure. He ambled toward the hounds and bent among them, pushing them aside and peering into the den. As he looked up he saw a man coming toward him, a young man in a monk's habit, clutching a dagger. He stood and stared as the monk closed the gate leading from the viaduct and moved forward.

Damien turned and saw another monk, gray-bearded, ride onto the viaduct, saw him close the gate and urge the horse at a walking pace toward him. He too carried a dagger.

Damien stiffened. So they had trapped him. He could not understand how they had done it. How had they known where the fox would go? But there was no time for speculation. They were closing in on him, front and back.

He glanced down at the hounds milling around him. Looking up, he caught the smile of triumph on the bearded monk's face. He was less than ten yards away. Damien switched his gaze to the horse, staring at it without blinking, summoning up all his powers of concentration. He imagined a chase, jackals chasing a horse; they caught up with it, nipping at its hooves, leaping at its hindquarters until it had been forced to its knees. A leg snapped so that it could not move . . . and then they had gone for its belly, gnawing and chewing at the soft entrails while the horse screamed, watching with dimmed eyes as they tore at its living flesh.

The mare stopped in its tracks, ignoring Antonio's urging. Its eyes widened and it tossed its head, but it could not escape Damien's stare. Quite unexpectedly, it reared high, sending Antonio slithering off its back and onto the parapet. For an instant his body balanced, then it tipped over, his hands scratching at air, the scream rising in his throat. And then he vanished.

Damien turned quickly. The young monk had stopped a few yards away. His face was white with horror as he peered over the parapet into the gorge. The screaming had stopped now. He looked back at Damien, the hand holding the dagger steady as he moved forward into the pack of hounds.

Damien did not move. He merely shifted his gaze to the biggest of the hounds, concentrating again. This time the image in his mind was different. The dog stared at him, his head cocked to one side, panting, its eyes narrowing. It stood motionless for a moment, then turned. Simeon was a yard from it. Without hesitation it leaped for his throat. It missed and snapped at his shoulder, tearing a rent in his cassock. Simeon dropped the dagger, stepped back, and gazed stupefied at the blood which oozed from the gash. He touched his shoulder and frowned. Briefly all was still; the two men and the hounds stood motionless as if frozen in a tableau. Then a second dog jumped on the young monk's back, its claws digging for a hold, the jaw reaching for the back of his neck. Simeon staggered backward, and the dog howled as it was crushed against the parapet wall, but now a third dog went for him, and a fourth. He fought them, kicking and punching, grabbing one dog by the throat and forcing its jaws shut. It squealed and fell back, but yet another snapped at him, ducked under his elbow, and butted him in the chest. He tripped and fell, his arms thrashing, his yells smothered by their bodies as they clambered over him.

Damien timed the struggle. It lasted exactly a minute and a half until one of the hounds found the throat and tore it open. They were crazed with blood now and ripped at him long after he had stopped moving.

For the hounds, the morning had not been wasted.

Back at the house, Peter was grumbling at his mother.

"Damien must have gone after another fox," he said. "Ours went over a waterfall."

Kate shrugged. "I think I'd rather be drowned than torn to shreds." She smiled at him. "Personally, that is."

He grinned back at her. They had the same sense of humor. It was something that would be valuable in the difficult adolescent years. She squeezed his hand, but he was looking over her shoulder and pointing. She turned to see Damien riding toward them, the hounds trailing behind, blood on their muzzles.

Peter kicked at his pony's flanks and rode to meet him.

"You caught one," he said as he closed the gap.

"The hounds didn't leave too many souvenirs," said Damien. "But I saved you some of the blood."

He reached into his pocket and drew out a blood-soaked handkerchief.

"Can you blood me?" Peter asked, looking up at him. "I mean, does it count?"

"It does with me," said Damien. He bent down and smeared the blood on the boy's cheeks. Peter touched his face, looked at the blood on his fingers, and pressed them to his lips.

Damien and Peter gazed at each other in silence, oblivious to their surrounding; a gaze of mutual understanding.

A hundred yards away Kate watched them, and she did not like what she saw.

14

Throughout the long drive to Cornwall, Frank Hutchins fed his excitement and stoked up his anticipation. He wanted to be the first to arrive, to be right at the front and to see him, to get as close as possible. Maybe he would be allowed to meet him, to receive a blessing for all the work he had done. After all, it was he who had gotten them all together. He was a vital cog in the machine, and with luck Damien Thorn would acknowledge him in some small way.

The last three hours he traveled in darkness, and when he reached the spot, he was glad to see that there were no other cars. He was early. He would be first. He locked the car and moved down the path toward the cove. It was a walk of half a mile, and before he reached it he could hear the waves on the rocky shore and see the beacon flashing across the horizon.

He reached the spot and stared out to sea, then began to clamber down the cliff toward the shore. The night was black and starless, and twice he nearly slipped. When he reached the bottom he looked back at the cliffs rearing two hundred feet on three sides of the cove. It was a wonderful black spot, and the excitement grew in him so that he could feel his heartbeat and the throbbing in his temples. He turned to see the first of the disciples make their way toward him, little flashes of light from their torches; three, four, then another group and another. He felt proud of himself, and he began to arrange them in ranks up the cliff, introducing himself as he moved among them.

And now it was almost time. He stood on the beach next to a young nurse and gazed around him. Each of them was staring out to sea, a thousand upturned faces caught for an instant in the flash of the beacon, a thousand white specks like gulls on the face of the cliff.

"There it is," Nurse Lamont whispered to him, and he looked out to the horizon, hearing the whine of the rotor blades before he saw the landing light. He stiffened with excitement as the big black helicopter moved toward them and hovered on the shore fifty yards away. He wanted to move forward, but the orders had to be obeyed, and so he stood where he was.

He could see him now, framed in the doorway of the machine. Hutchins gasped, and he felt the nurse move close to him, felt her hand touch his, and then Damien jumped to the shore and stood motionless as the helicopter lifted again, veered out to sea, and vanished.

Once more there was silence. Damien waited, a solitary dark figure by the shore, and then he raised his arms.

"Disciples of the Watch," he shouted. "I stand before you in the name of the one true God, Lord of the Lower Empire, who was cast out of heaven but is alive in me."

He paused, then quietly spoke again. "Do you hear me?"

Every man, woman, and child answered in a monotone, "We hear and obey."

The beacon light swung across the cliff, illuminating the awed faces gazing toward him. Hutchins caught a glimpse of the nurse's expression, the excitement in her eyes, her lips wet.

"I now command you," said Damien, "to seek out and destroy the Nazarene child."

The nurse moved closer to Hutchins and grasped his hand.

"Slay the Nazarene and I reign forever. Fail and I perish."

"No," she whispered. "I will not fail."

"Slay the Nazarene and you, my disciples, inherit the earth. Fail and you perish without a trace. Slay the Nazarene and you will know the violent raptures of my father's paradise hereafter."

Her grip tightened on Hutchins's hand, and he could feel her body pressed against his.

"Fail and you will be condemned to a numbing eternity in the flaccid bosom of Christ."

Again he shouted, "Do you hear me?"

"We hear and obey"—louder this time.

"Disciples of the Watch. There must be no delay. Slay the Nazarene and victory shall be ours, now and forevermore. Do you hear me?"

"We hear and obey."

Damien stood before them, and the chant rose around him as if rehearsed: "Slay the Nazarene. Slay the Nazarene . . ." The chorus drifted out to sea and into the dark night sky.

As he shouted the words, Hutchins drew the nurse toward him, and she grabbed at him, wrestling with him, tearing at his clothes. The sex was violent and brief, the two of them grappling with one another, oblivious to the others, unaware that others were doing the same and the children were watching . . . and even as the orgasm wracked his body he heard her voice above the others, shouting his name, "Damien, I love you," but he felt no jealousy, for he was screaming the same words.

15

Almost from the start, Barbara Dean had fallen in love with London. The house in Hampstead was so charming, with its cozy rooms and walled garden. She could not wait till the summer, when the flowers would be in bloom and she could show her new friends how she could fix a barbecue. The streets were so pretty, the lanes narrow and full of character. She loved the antique shops and the pubs, and she thought the people were wonderful. Maybe some of her new friends were a little snooty and aloof. Occasionally she thought that perhaps they were making fun of her. What was Harvey's word? She searched her memory and dredged it up. Supercilious. That was it. Maybe they were supercilious, but that was okay. That was the way they were supposed to be, the English; aloof and supercilious. She would have been disappointed if they had been any different.

Hampstead was definitely tops with Barbara Dean,

especially now that she was a mother. It would be such a nice place to bring up the baby.

She was singing to herself as she made out her shopping list. When she had finished, she checked in her purse for money and credit cards, then moved to the cot, picked up the baby, and kissed and tickled it. The baby cooed happily as she placed him in his pram. She turned as she heard a tap at the window. A woman her own age was standing outside; an English rose, Harvey called her, blond and pink-cheeked.

"Hi, Carol," she said, waving. "I'll be right with you."

She wrapped a blanket around the baby, smoothed his hair down, moved to the door, and shouted up the stairs.

"Harvey?"

"Yeah?" Dean's voice was faint.

"I'm going shopping with Carol."

"Okay."

"I'm taking the baby with me."

"Okay."

Singing again, she turned and pushed the pram into the front garden. Carol's pram was parked by the gate, and she pushed hers next to it. The women looked down adoringly at the babies, who gurgled back at them.

"Could be twins," said Carol.

"Well, they are," said Barbara. "More or less."

"More or less," Carol repeated, giggling at something. Barbara looked at her and laughed along with her.

"After you," she said.

"No," said Carol. "After you."

Giggling like a couple of schoolgirls, they strolled

off into the sunshine along the avenue, pushing their prams before them.

Dean watched them go and then returned to his desk. Papers were strewn across it. Carefully he shuffled them together into a tidy pile. They were photocopies of birth certificates. Hutchins had done his job well. He was known by the clerk at the Records Office, and no one had questioned him when he had gone in to look at the files. The man had assumed that the young barrister was about his legitimate business. Dean leafed through the papers. Hutchins had been thorough, and he could not have known that there was one name missing; Harvey Dean Junior's birth certificate was not on the list, for the simple reason that Harvey Dean Senior had gotten there first. For a few minutes he checked each one off against a list, then he reached into his briefcase and took out a radiotelephone.

He took a deep breath, closed his eyes for a moment, then tapped out a number.

"Peterson?" he said. "Harvey Dean."

He paused, then brushed aside the other man's small talk. There was no time for it, and he was not in the mood. "You are operating OS sections, sectors TQ 1423 through TS 2223. Is that right? . . . Okay. You have three in Liverpool."

He picked up the first three photocopies and read out the addresses. When he had finished, he hit the button and tapped out another number.

The two women had taken their time with the shopping, but now they were finished, the groceries piled at the foot of the prams, their babies peering over the carrier bags. Barbara's boy had fallen asleep, but Carol's was awake, gazing around him, gurgling and spitting.

In a lane off Hampstead High Street they stopped outside a pub. Carol went inside and came out with two glasses of lager, and they stood sipping their drinks in the spring sunshine, Barbara feeling wicked, making jokes about turning into an alcoholic, giving a bad impression to their sons. When she had finished she looked at her watch and then remembered the British custom of buying rounds of drinks.

"You want the other half?" she asked.

Carol shook her head. She had to get back. They left in opposite directions, waving to one another, lifting the babies' hands and waggling their fingers at each other.

For a moment Carol watched Barbara make her way across the road. She was so sweet, she thought, so innocent somehow, yet so intense at other times, and often she did not understand when the others were being flippant. She took things at face value. But it was no criticism. Barbara Dean was a good friend to have, the sort of person you could rely on, and better by half than that husband of hers. She laughed to herself at the memory of their first meeting at a party and the clumsy pass he had made at her. Poor Barbara, to be saddled with such a man.

As she set off for home, she recalled the day she had met Barbara, the two of them side by side in the nursing home, and how they had laughed when they had discovered that they were due on the same day. Ever since, they had called the boys twins, Barbara's the older by just forty minutes.

The baby burped, and she smiled at him. She bent and tickled his chin. He flailed an arm, knocking his bottle over the side of the pram.

"Naughty," she said, stepping on the brake and bending to retrieve it from the gutter. It had picked up a speck of dirt, and she dropped it into her bag. There she released the brake and set off once more. The baby gurgled at her and waved its arms.

"Simon James Fraser," she said. "Behave yourself."

In reply Simon spat at her, and she laughed aloud. She had never been happier. In two months Tony would be free for a month, and they had rented a villa at Corfu. They would lie on the beach like lizards and soak up the sun.

"You'll get fat and brown," she told her son. "Fat Simon."

One pink foot escaped from the blanket as she turned the pram down the hill. She leaned forward and tickled it. The baby squealed, his head slipping deeper into the pillows as the pram tilted on the steep grade.

She stopped with a start as something suddenly dropped in front of her, bumping her shoulder. She screamed as it swung away from her and back toward her face—a gray squirrel, its throat cut, the eyes gouged from their sockets, hanging upside down with a length of string tied around its back legs.

Instinctively her hands fluttered to her mouth as she screamed, then leaped forward, pushing the squirrel aside. The pram trundled away from her down the hill.

Carol leaped for the handle but missed. She ran, trying to kick off the high-heeled shoes, but tripped on them as the pram picked up speed. Whimpering, she stumbled after it and tripped over her feet, going down on her knees, scrabbling up again and running knock-kneed down the hill, refusing to accept the obvious, that she would never catch up.

She was still running when the pram reached the foot of the hill. It bounced off the pavement onto the main road, and she could not even close her eyes as the truck smashed into it, kept running as the wheels crushed the pram as if it were a cardboard box. ...

Behind her, in the trees, the squirrel was drawn up into the branches, and the boy, Trevor Grant, laughed, congratulating himself on the success of his scheme.

It had been a difficult birth. The mother had had a narrow pelvis, and the baby was born prematurely, by Caesarean section. But she had recovered quickly after she saw the boy in its incubator in the intensive-care ward. He weighed only five pounds, but the doctors told her that he was quite healthy. It was just a matter of time. She was to go home and visit as often as she wanted, and she was not to worry.

He lay asleep in his oxygen tent, one of twelve tiny patients in the hospital's Special Baby Care Unit. The doctors and nurses were proud of the unit. Since it had been set up, the infant mortality rate in the county had halved.

Two nurses, wearing masks and gowns, made a final check of their patients before leaving for a tea break. Satisfied, they left the ward, stripping off their masks at the door. As they reached the end of the corridor, Nurse Lamont walked smartly past them, unrecognizable through her mask. She waited until the others had gone, then pushed open the door of the ward. But for the hiss of oxygen, the room was silent. She moved to the first cot, checked the name on the chart, then moved to the next and the next until she found the baby she wanted.

Curious, she glanced at him. He had put on two

pounds since birth. His face had lost its pinched look, the arms were becoming quite chubby, and his breathing was regular. Stretching to her left, she twisted the oxygen valve, walked away, and waited by the window. Two minutes later she returned, switched on the oxygen once more, and looked down. The baby was still.

As she looked down at the child in her arms, the woman gave thanks to God. Twice she had suffered miscarriages, and if this third pregnancy had failed, then there would have been no other chance. But he was gorgeous, all nine pounds of him, with his father's eyes and chin. He was going to play for England, his dad had promised, and at that moment, in the church where she herself had been baptized and married, she thought that he would be able to do whatever he wanted. He would be given every chance. No sacrifice would be too much.

All around her, voices sang in praise:

"The sun shall not burn thee by day, nor the moon by night. The Lord keepeth thee from all evil; may the Lord keep thy soul. . . ."

She looked at the choirboys, up at her husband, then back at her parents and up at the vicar. They were all singing lustily.

"May the Lord keep thy coming in and thy going out, henceforth now and forevermore."

She looked into the boy's face and joined in the amen. Behind her, the godparents moved forward so that they were grouped around the font.

"Dearly beloved," said the Reverend Graham Ross, "ye have brought this child here to be baptized. I demand therefore, do ye, in the name of this child, renounce the devil and all his works, so that ye will not follow nor be led by them?"

"We renounce them all," said the godparents.

The vicar stepped forward and held out his arms. The mother looked again into her baby's face, then handed him over to the vicar. As he cradled the baby in his left arm, the mother grasped her husband's hand.

"I name this child . . ." the vicar began.

"Alexander David," the mother said softly.

The vicar took the baby to the edge of the font.

"I baptize thee Alexander David, in the name of the Father, of the Son, and of the Holy Ghost. Amen."

He turned, held the baby's head with his left hand, dipped the fingers of his right hand in the font, and sprinkled the baby's face with water. The baby squealed and blinked, curled up his nose, and began to wail.

The mother smiled at her husband as the vicar turned away from them.

"We receive this child into the congregation of Christ's flock and do sign him with the sign of the Cross. . . ."

The vicar's strong fingers probed the baby's skull, searching for the soft pulsing cleft where the bone had not yet closed. He found it, and the baby stopped crying.

High in her apartment in a public housing project, the young mother was nearing the end of her tether. The vandals had broken the elevators again. Her man was at sea and was not due back for a month, and the baby would not shut up. The sound of its wailing was getting on her nerves, and the milk had boiled over, putting out the gas.

She had tried counting to a hundred. She had tried coaxing the baby to sleep. She had tried bullying, and the threat of grievous bodily harm. But still the noise echoed around the flat until she felt like jumping out of the window.

The bell chimed, that dreadful sequence from *The Sound of Music* that her man was so proud of and that drove her crazy.

Grumbling, she padded to the door and opened it.

Two Cub Scouts looked up at her, smiling sweetly.

"Good morning, missus," said one. "We've come to do our good deed for the day."

She looked at them in silence for a moment.

"Has either of you got any baby brothers or sisters?"

"Yes, missus," said the smaller one.

"Do you know how to take care of babies?"

"Yes, missus. I take care of my sister when my mum's out."

"Wait there," she said and turned toward the baby, thanking God for the Boy Scout movement. She put the baby in its pram and wheeled it back to the door.

Maybe now, she thought, I'll get a bit of peace.

16

Spring had turned sour for Barbara Dean. At first when Tony had phoned with the news, she had not believed it. When it had sunk in, she fainted. When she came around, she cried for an hour, then went around to the house, but Carol was under sedation and remained so for two days. On the third day Barbara was allowed into the bedroom, and the two women clung to one another, sobbing, their tears mingling. And now she had developed a routine. Each morning she went to the house, bringing sympathy. There was nothing she could say, only clichés, but she hoped that just by being there, she helped in some small way.

As soon as she had heard the news, she had banished the pram to the garage and sworn never to use it. Now she carried her child everywhere; it meant that she had only one hand to use when shopping, but she did not care. A friend offered her a baby bag, a canvas knapsack which held the baby against the mother's back, but Barbara refused even that. The strap might break. The baby might slip through the bottom. No, she would carry the child in her arms. It was the only safe way.

Instinctively she turned to Harvey for help, crying in his arms at night and babbling incoherently. It was her fault, she said. She should never have agreed to stand drinking outside the pub. If only she had said no, then maybe . . .

Harvey tried to quiet her, but even in her sleep she kept seeing her son in his pram careening down the hill, and she would wake up screaming.

During the day she was forgetful. She would find herself in the bedroom and wonder why she had climbed the stairs. She would cook a stew and forget to put in the salt. And Harvey was not much help. Lately he had become distant and preoccupied. Everything had gone wrong, and she was beginning to hate London.

That night over dinner they had scarcely said a word, Harvey morosely watching television as she fed the baby.

They watched a Western through to the credits, then Harvey grunted something under his breath as the program changed.

"*World in Focus*, presented by Kate Reynolds."

Idly Barbara wondered why he did not seem to like the woman commentator. She had seemed pleasant enough at the reception; a bit pushy, perhaps, but then she needed to be, in her job. Maybe Harvey was scared of her. Like many men he shied away from aggressive women as if they carried the plague.

"Good evening," said Kate, smiling at them. Harvey rose from his chair to switch the set off.

"Tonight we're devoting the first part of our program to a bizarre phenomenon that has been puzzling police and doctors alike during the last week. . . ."

He reached for the button.

". . . the mysterious deaths of dozens of baby boys . . ."

"Wait," said Barbara, sitting up. Harvey shrugged and stood by the set, looking down at it.

". . . the deaths occurring in the kind of circumstances coroners are fond of terming 'misadventure.'"

"Sit down, Harvey. I can't see," Barbara said sharply, and Harvey did as he was asked, picked up his wine glass, and sipped from it.

"In Greater London alone," Kate continued, "seventeen boys have died in the past seven days, while in the provinces, Birmingham reports six dead, Liverpool three, Manchester four, Leeds two, Glasgow eight."

Barbara frowned and stared intently at the screen.

"These may not sound like unduly high figures, but nationwide they represent a chilling fifteen percent rise in the infant mortality rate. Details are still sketchy at the moment, and no clear pattern has yet emerged. Except one." Kate paused, the screen changing to closeup. "In every case, the victim has been a baby boy."

Barbara stiffened, the breath caught in her throat. She clutched her baby tight. Dean turned at the sound of his wife's gasp and looked at her. He wanted to go to her, tell her that it was okay, that he was in charge and their baby was safe. But he could say nothing, and so he turned back to the set. Kate was introducing a spokesman for the Ministry of Health and Social Security.

"Tell me, Dr. Philmore," she said, "what explanation can you offer at this stage?"

The man shuffled in his seat and shrugged his shoulders. "Well, of course, it's too soon for us to make any definite statement at—"

Kate leaned forward, interrupting him. "But you do admit there's been a totally unexplained rise in deaths among baby boys over the past week?"

"A rise, yes indeed, but nothing compared to the rise you'd expect to find during, say, a flu epidemic."

The camera switched to Kate and caught her scornful expression.

"But we're not talking about an epidemic," she said sharply. "We're talking about"—ticking off points on her fingers—"drownings, household burns, car accidents, suffocation, food poisoning, electrocution . . ." She paused, trying to think back to the list she had read only ten minutes earlier, and Philmore hungrily leaped into the silence.

"You'll forgive me if I speak bluntly," he said. "But your kind of scaremonger reporting is exactly the kind of behavior that brings the media into disrepute. It really is a gross irresponsibility to start exaggerating the facts in order to get yourself a story that even the lowest Sunday newspaper would think twice about before printing."

Again the camera caught Kate's expression. She sat open-mouthed and at a loss for words.

Dean glanced at his wife. She was still frowning, still clutching the baby to her as if it were about to shatter into tiny pieces. Dr. Philmore had been good, he thought, which was why he had been picked for the program. He had given his best shot, but he hadn't convinced Barbara, for one. He only hoped that he had convinced the rest of the country.

"So what went wrong with you?" The young program director's voice was sharp and accusing, the words spat at her.

"I'm sorry, Bob, I just didn't expect . . ." Kate said.

"You let him go on with that old garbage."

"I told you," Kate snapped back, "it was unexpected. Totally. I'd no idea he would act so defens—"

"Crap, Kate," the director shouted, his spittle spraying the room. He snapped his fingers. "Like that, you have to be. Sharp, incisive. Don't let the bastards get away with anything." He turned and stalked out of the room, leaving Kate cursing silently behind him.

"Hopped-up young Cambridge know-it-all," she muttered. She would like to see him out there under the lights. It was easy to criticize from the sidelines. But of course he was right, and the knowledge did nothing to improve her mood. She should never have let Philmore dive into the attack like that. She simply was caught off guard. It wasn't as if *she* were attacking *him*. It wasn't as if it were his *fault* that the babies were dead. It was crazy. She had built her reputation on aggressive interviewing, but that was when she was attacking obvious targets—people who had to defend their own or their department's incompetence or negligence, people who had something to cover up or feel guilty about.

So, why was he so aggressive? She thought about it and came up with no answer. Maybe his wife was frigid. Maybe he had an impacted wisdom tooth. Who could tell? She decided that she would have a drink or two at the club and forget all about it.

She got home late, annoyed with herself. Normally she picked Peter up from the sitter's flat downstairs, but now it was too late. He would have gone on upstairs to bed by now. She parked the car and climbed the front steps, scuffling in her bag for the key, cursing herself for being a bad mother, for letting her job get the better of her duty to her son.

"Miss Reynolds."

The voice startled her, a deep voice at her elbow. She turned and stared into the face of a priest.

"I need to talk to you urgently, Miss Reynolds."

She sighed irritably. The phone book, she thought. It was about time to be unlisted. She was becoming too well known; too many strangers could just walk up to her front door.

"About your program. About the deaths."

"A protest march of one," she said sarcastically. "How disappointing."

"On the contrary," said Father De Carlo. "I congratulate you. You have been very perceptive."

She leaned back against the door, her key in her hand.

"Well?" she said, watching as the priest glanced up and down the street. What was coming next?

"May we talk inside?"

She shook her head. "I'm sorry—"

"My name is Father De Carlo. I am a priest."

"I've had a long day, Father," Kate said wearily. "If you'd like to call my secretary at the studio and make an appointment."

"It's a matter of the utmost urgency, Miss Reynolds."

She stared at him. He did not look as if he would be any trouble. Certainly he seemed sincere enough. Okay, she thought, let the man have his say and then he'll be satisfied.

She pushed the door open and stood back to let him in.

"But keep your voice down," she said. "My son's asleep."

She ushered him into the living room. As usual it was a mess; books, papers, cardboard files everywhere. She was about to apologize for the mess, and then, she thought to hell with it. Let him take it or leave it. It wasn't as if he had been invited. She gestured toward an armchair and took her coat off as he sat down. As she was about to ask him to explain himself, he looked at the ceiling and launched into a quotation.

" 'Then Herod sent forth and slew all the children that were in Bethlehem, and in all the coasts thereof, according to the time of the birth of Jesus, which he had diligently inquired of the wise men.' "

Kate groaned. "What on earth . . . ?"

Father De Carlo held up his hand to pacify her and continued. "You said on your program that the common factor in these killings is that all the victims have been baby boys."

Kate nodded.

"But there is another common factor, Miss Reynolds. All the boys were born between midnight and six a.m. on the morning of March twenty-fourth. Any boy still living, born between those hours, is in mortal danger, if indeed he has not already been done to death."

Done to death, thought Kate. What fine old-fashioned words. This one was a character for sure. She decided to humor him for a moment.

"You're suggesting they've been murdered."

"No. I'm stating it as a fact."

"But who on earth would want to do such a thing?"

Father De Carlo leaned forward, and she was aware of the repressed excitement in him. His hands were shaking, his eyes were bright, and he looked as though he had not slept for a month. For the first time Kate began to feel concerned. Maybe the man was mad.

"He is born again, Miss Reynolds. And so is the Anti-Christ, the Son of Satan, as foretold in the Book of Revelations."

"I'm sorry, Father," she said, rising to her feet. "I respect your faith, but I don't share it." She could have kicked herself, letting this crazy man into her flat. He would have to go.

"You're not a practicing Christian?" he asked.

"I'm a practicing journalist," she replied. "And the first rule in journalism is to be a Doubting Thomas. I need to see evidence with my own eyes."

And now she had given him another chance. He opened his briefcase. Again Kate groaned inwardly as he pulled out a sheaf of papers and handed them over.

"Here is your evidence. Check for yourself."

Reluctantly she took them and laid them on her desk. They were copies of birth certificates. Her eyes narrowed as she recognized the names.

"I got them from the Central Registry Office," he said, as if needing to explain.

She looked up at him and allowed him to continue.

"Even if I can't appeal to your faith, I appeal to your logic. Why else would someone want to kill every boy born on that date, if it were not in an effort to destroy one child in particular?"

Her instinct began to gnaw at her. Not murder surely, but she knew by experience that coincidence needed to be investigated, Son of Satan or no Son of Satan.

"And who is this Anti-Christ?" she asked.

"The American Ambassador. Damien Thorn."

She looked at him briefly, then squealed with laughter.

"Damien," she said, trying to control herself. It was the height of bad manners to laugh in someone's face, especially someone as serious as this priest. "But I know Damien," she said weakly.

"You know the man," De Carlo said. "But not his soul."

He leaned forward and took her hand.

"Miss Reynolds," he said, his voice quiet, talking slowly as if to a child. "I am a religious man, not a fanatic. One of the commandments of our faith is that we not bear false witness against any man. If I held one shred of doubt about Damien Thorn, my faith would command me to remain silent."

Kate was forced to gaze into his face. She was serious now, entranced by his quiet sincerity. So intent was she on his words, and his need to explain, that neither of them heard Peter tiptoe along the corridor; nor did they see him stand half hidden by the doorway.

"I have watched Thorn for twenty-seven years," he continued, "ever since his father came to our monastery to seek help in destroying him. I have watched him grow into a man and seen him exterminate all those who stood in his way."

Peter moved back into the shadows, listening intently.

"You know Thorn the man, Miss Reynolds." He stood up and took out a file from his briefcase. "I will leave you with our research on him, but you must satisfy yourself before reaching your opinion. When you have done so, I would urge you to contact me at this address." He wrote on the file. "Do it as soon as possible, day or night."

Kate took the file and looked up at him. "I can't promise you anything, Father," she said. "You say I know only Damien the man, not his soul. But if I don't know my own soul, how can I see into his?"

"Only God can show you that." Father De Carlo said, smiling, relieved that the woman's initial skepticism was at least partly allayed. He snapped his fingers. Of course. He had almost forgotten to mention the one thing that might convince her.

"There is one outward sign that identifies him. You will find it in the Book of Revelations. You will also find it on Thorn himself, under his hair, the birthmark of the Devil: three sixes."

He took her hand and pressed it and wished her goodnight.

"May God guide you in your decision," he said and moved to the door as Peter scurried silently back to his room.

When he had gone, Kate took the file to her bedroom, her mind a confused mixture of disbelief and curiosity. The man's suggestions were, of course, insane. But she would read his notes just to satisfy the itch in her brain. She lay on the bed and flipped through the pages.

He had underlined the appointment as president of the Youth Council and had made a few comments. As she read it, Kate was reminded of Damien's words at the interview: how he wanted to help young people gain a more prominent role in world affairs. She remembered his passion, the way he had launched into a speech. And she remembered the old saying, "Give me a boy till he is six and I shall have him always"—something like that. She shivered, thinking of Peter at the hunt, the blood smeared on his face.

Father De Carlo had included a Thorn Corporation

brochure with its listings of the countries being given relief. And he had added a rider: "U.S. President by the age of forty?"

Kate stretched out, trying to clear her mind. Gullibility was the cardinal sin of journalism. Yet skepticism was the easiest route of all to take. She remembered her first boss, an editor on the local evening paper, warning her, telling her that the words "what a load of rubbish" made up the easiest sentence in the English language. It was easy to scoff.

But it was, wasn't it? Rubbish? The whole thing was crazy. She was weary and the man had taken advantage of her exhaustion to promote all this . . . rubbish.

Damien Thorn, the Son of Satan. It was absurd. She turned over and fell instantly asleep in her clothes, and she did not see or hear Peter come in, pick up the file, and stare at the address on the cover.

17

Harvey Dean recognized the symptoms. He was in danger of becoming a basket case, frightened of his dreams but scared to wake up. He was wary of going to work and edgy when he was in Damien's presence. He had tried to work out solutions to the problem, but there were none. There was nowhere to go. He had to sit tight and hope for the best. His future was out of his hands, his happiness at the mercy of another.

The trouble was that he had discovered that he was crazy about his son. He loved everything about him, from the toylike toenails to the spiky hair. He loved the baby more than he loved Barbara and more than he loved Damien. But if he ran, if he took the baby away, then eventually he would be found. His running would be proof of his disloyalty, and that, in the eyes of Damien Thorn, was the worst crime of all.

And if all that were not bad enough, the Israeli operation was going down the tubes as well.

He grunted into the phone and looked across at Damien.

"The Israelis are on to Schroeder," he said. "We've got to eliminate him now before they can make him talk."

Damien did not look up from his papers. "Then do it." he said.

"We can't get close to him," Dean said, no longer attempting to keep the exasperation from his voice. "He's being held in Tel Aviv. You're the only one who can do it, Damien."

"You can take care of it."

"But I just told you—"

"And I told *you*," Damien said, looking up at last and staring at Dean, his eyes stabbing at him, "I told you before that my force would weaken for every day that the Nazarene lives."

Dean swallowed hard. Why had he not kept his mouth shut? They were back to that subject again. Just do as he says, he told himself. Don't make waves.

"How many boys are left?" asked Damien.

"Only one or two." Please drop it, he pleaded silently.

"Including your son."

"My son?" he said too quickly. "Now wait just a minute. I already told you that he was born March twenty-third. Believe me, Damien, he is—"

"Destroy the Nazarene. Then I'll believe you."

The phone rang, and Dean grabbed at it, relieved, feeling like a drowning man reaching for an oar. The oar was making bleeping noises, and he frowned. Who would be phoning from a booth? How did they get through?

"Yes?" He looked puzzled. "Who?"

He turned to Damien. "It's Kate Reynolds' son. In a booth."

Damien stood and moved toward him.

"How did he get the number?" Dean asked.

"Because I gave it to him."

Dean shrugged, cursing his perpetual curiosity. It would kill him one day.

He pretended not to listen. What did it matter if Damien was asking the brat to follow somebody? What concern was it of his that the child should make sure not to be seen?

Damien hung up and Dean was quickly at him, making sure that there was no return to the interrupted subject.

"Be careful, Damien. His mother was on the phone this morning wanting to see you. I managed to stall her, but—"

"Why didn't you tell me?" Damien snapped. "I wanted to talk to her."

"The woman's dangerous," Dean persisted. "Her television show has already stirred up enough—"

"*I* decide who's dangerous and who isn't," Damien said, his face dark with anger. "Now get her on the phone. Tell her I'll see her this afternoon up at the house. But don't mention anything about Peter."

Dean shrugged. "You're the boss," he said, as he made a note on his pad, and was relieved to see Damien stalk out of the office.

Dean left the office early that night, his mind clouded with fear and worry. He coaxed the car north through the early-evening traffic until he reached the hill and headed into the clear air of the Heath. He was glad to be going home, and he just wished that there were no telephone, no umbilical link to Damien Thorn. If only he could walk through the front door, close it behind him, and shut out the world. He and Barbara would go to bed early tonight, just after dinner. Maybe she was not the most intelligent woman in town, maybe she was a bit countrified and old-fashioned, but right then Dean did not mind. What he wanted was a night in bed with an old-fashioned, uncomplicated woman who loved him.

He parked the car in the garage, let himself in, and shouted up the stairs.

There was no reply. He checked the kitchen and the dining room. Maybe she had gone out. But she usually left him a note. He poured himself a drink and climbed the stairs to his study, pushed the door open, and stood motionless, gazing at the chaos in front of him.

Barbara was sitting in his chair, the baby on her lap. Papers were strewn all over the floor. His filing cabinet had been looted, drawers torn out and left lying open.

"What on earth?" he grunted and stepped forward. Barbara spun in the chair, clutched the baby to her, and screamed at him. Her face was twisted in hate, her eyes puffy with tears.

"Don't come anywhere near him!" she screamed. "Murderer!"

Dean stopped as if he had walked into a wall. He blinked.

"Have you gone crazy?"

He stepped forward again. Barbara reached for the letter knife on the desk and held it in front of her. Dean stopped, his face white with shock and anger.

"Lay one finger on him and I'll butcher you," said

his wife. "Just as you butchered all those innocent children."

He opened his mouth to protest but could say nothing.

"A priest came by this afternoon," she said. "He came to warn me about Damien Thorn. He told me who he was, that he will murder my baby just as he killed all the others born the same day."

Deny it, Dean thought; deny everything. Then he spoke, his voice hoarse.

"You mean you believe some religious maniac who—"

"No," she said, dropping the knife and scrabbling on the desk. "I found proof for myself." And she held up the copies of the birth certificates.

There was nothing more to be said. Dean shook his head and rubbed his face, blinking as if he had been struck hard. He looked lost and vulnerable. Barbara got to her feet, the tears flowing again, her anger gone.

"For the love of God, Harvey, you've got to help the priest destroy Damien." He looked up at her and finally nodded. Encouraged by his gesture, she rushed to him. "He says you can do it. Damien trusts you. Please, Harvey, get in touch with him. For the love of God, Harvey . . . for the love of our son."

He reached for her, and they stood together in the chaos of his study, rocking on their heels, the baby held between them, pulling Dean's hair.

18

When she was a child, Kate had consistently evoked the same response from relatives and friends of the family. She was so self-assured, they would say, so self-confident. The terms had applied throughout her adolescence, when she left home to live in London and Paris, where she happily and quite without guilt slept with strangers. It was Kate who picked Frank for her husband, to the unanimous delight of her family.

When he died they expected her to crack, for it was the first tragedy of her life, but no one saw her in tears. Since then there had been three men in her life. Kate had chosen, enjoyed, and rejected each of them. She told them about Frank but did not permit them access to her grief.

After the relationships had changed, Kate kept each of them as a friend, saying often that one test of maturity was the ability to remain on good terms with ex-lovers. There were occasions, in the fevered lone-liness of the night, when she wished that she could meet someone with whom it would be impossible to be friendly afterward, to have an emotional cloud-burst, a love affair of such intensity that they would need to part forever. But in the mornings she dis-missed these thoughts as romantic nonsense, sentimen-tal indulgence.

Self-controlled, self-assured, professional; until she met Damien Thorn.

She awakened that morning clutching at the frag-ments of a dream. For a moment she did not know where she was, and then she remembered the crazy priest and his insane theories. At breakfast she tried to concentrate on the papers and the early-morning radio news programs, but Father De Carlo's words kept in-truding.

As soon as she got to her desk, she rang the em-bassy. Quite what she was going to say she did not know; she would just have to play it by ear. But the problem was resolved for her. He was not in. She left a message and tried to forget him, going through her mail and checking her diary, but still she could not focus her attention on anything. Her brain felt like a banjo, and badly tuned at that. After half an hour she gave up. It was no good. She itched with curiosity, and there was nothing to do but scratch. Snapping her diary shut, she left her desk, climbed two floors to the library, and asked for the file on Damien Thorn.

The male librarian grimaced. "Not having him on again, are you?"

She smiled.

"I'll put in for an asbestos suit if you decide to have him on again. . . ."

She nodded at him, her smile intact. They always

had to have their little joke, and you had to be polite or else they would keep you waiting till the end of the week.

She began with the earliest clipping, a short account of a young woman named Chessa, Damien's nanny, who had hanged herself during a garden party at Pereford. She had jumped off the roof with a rope around her neck. It had been Damien's fourth birthday. The newspaper clipping was somewhat yellow, and as Kate read it, the paper crackled faintly in her hands. She shuddered and flipped through, turned to the next. Mrs. Kathy Thorn, wife of the U.S. Ambassador, badly hurt in a fall in the country mansion. She had been pregnant and she had lost the baby.

Kate frowned, flipped over: Kathy Thorn dead, a mysterious accident as she fell from a window in the hospital.

"My God," she breathed.

Robert Thorn she knew about, of course. It was all part of the Thorn tragedy. There were other innocuous stories about the expansion of the Thorn financial empire. Then, datelined Boston, came the story of one of Richard Thorn's chief executives, William Atherton, drowned during a weekend at the Thorn mansion. He had fallen, said the clipping, through the ice during a game of hockey. Then again, David Pasarian, chief of agricultural research at Thorn Industries, dead after an accident while pupils from Damien's school were being conducted around the plant. This was a short piece compared to the others, as if the news editors of the time had not given it much importance.

Kate winced and looked at a speck of blood on her finger. She had been biting her nails. When was the last time she had bitten her nails? As a child perhaps, if then.

Fascinated, despite herself, she continued. Damien's cousin Mark, dead at the age of thirteen; a mysterious collapse; the autopsy showed an artery wall had burst in his skull.

"Thirteen," she said quietly. "A year older than Peter."

She could go on no longer, she had read enough.

She grimaced, wiped her fingers, went to the washroom to wash her hands. Death and destruction, she thought, tragedy and mystery, accidents and deaths without apparent cause. The corpse in the studio had never been identified. It was just one more enigma.

"Kate!"

She turned to see her assistant at the door.

"Someone called Harvey Dean just phoned from the American Embassy. Says the Ambassador will see you at his country house this afternoon."

She thanked her and dried her hands, aware of the excitement building inside her. It was absurd. Acting like a schoolgirl going to her first dance. She poked out her tongue at the mirror and heard herself whistling as she went back to her desk.

Again she looked at her diary. If she went to Pereford she would need to postpone two meetings. It could be done. They could wait, and if need be she could justify the trip to her producer on the grounds of additional research. She could con him, but she could not con herself. There was no reason to go to see Damien Thorn, no professional reason. She was going because he wanted to see her. It was as simple as that.

As she drove through the suburbs of West London,

she sang along with the radio station and answered the questions on the quiz, but when she reached the highway, the sound of the engine drowned out the radio. She switched it off and began anticipating her conversation with Damien.

"A priest came to see me last night," she said to herself, talking aloud.

"Really?"

"He said you were the Son of Satan."

"Satan who?"

She giggled to herself.

"Did you hear about the baby deaths?"

"Yes."

"Did you know that they were all born between midnight and six on March twenty-fourth?"

"Well, well, isn't that something?"

She shook her head.

"You seem to be something of a Jonah."

"Who? Me? How come?"

"People die all around you. . . ."

She laughed again, but now the mirth was forced. The burned corpse forced its way back into her memory, and for an instant she thought of turning back. If she had any sense she would steer clear of Damien Thorn. But the idea passed as quickly as it had arrived, and she drove on quietly and carefully, lost in thought, turned off at the proper exit and drove along a secondary road to the village.

At the gate the security man waved her through, saying she was expected, and as she skidded to a halt on the gravel, George appeared in the doorway, bowing to her and ushering her inside. She shivered as she got out of the car. It was colder than in town, the remnants of the night frost clinging to the verges.

"The Ambassador is in the study, ma'am," said George.

"Thank you." It would be nice to have a butler, she thought, a butler and a cook, a footman and a masseur and a chauffeur and . . .

"Kate, good of you to come." Damien came from behind his desk, kissed her lightly on the cheek. "Can I get you a drink?"

"No thanks. My head feels like a cabbage from the car heater."

"I can offer you some air, then," he said. "A quick tour of the estate."

"Fine."

She looked at him as he pulled on a suede jacket. It was the eyes, she thought, and the cheekbones. She wondered how many girls he had had in college, how many since, and why there was never any mention of them. As he zipped up his jacket he blinked and swallowed a yawn. Under his suntan he looked exhausted. She wondered why. She wanted to ask him but held back. It was none of her business. Yet he should not be so drained. The job of an ambassador was not particularly demanding; but perhaps it was the strain of doing two jobs. She remembered that he had dodged the question during the interview. No, he had said, there was no conflict of interest. If any conflict arose, then obviously he would resign.

But from which post? She had asked, and he had merely smiled as if the question were superfluous.

"Ready?" He held open the French windows, and she squeezed past him onto the terrace. They strolled through the gardens. As Damien pointed out to her the spots where he had played as a child, she glanced back at the house, wondering from which window the girl had hanged herself.

He led her to the rose garden and along the boundary of the lawn. Beneath them, over a fence, the ground sloped steeply toward the river. As she listened, she wondered when he would explain why he had invited her. For the moment he seemed content to act as host and guide.

At the fence they turned and looked back at the house.

"You know," he said, "if ever I became President of the United States, the first thing I'd do would be to move this place back to the U.S.A., lock, stock, and memories."

Kate scowled at him. "And I'd be the first to stop you," she said. "You've taken London Bridge." She spread the fingers of one hand and ticked off points. "You've taken the *Queen Mary*." She wavered, trying to think of something else, but she was stuck. "Soon we'll have nothing left but the fog, and even that is pretty thin on the ground these days."

Damien grinned at her.

"Anyway," she said, "why are you so fond of England?"

"Oh, I don't know," he said and shrugged. "I believe that one's heart lies where one's childhood lies. And mine is buried here. England is my land of lost content."

She looked up at him, wondering if he was being flippant, but he was gazing wistfully toward the house.

"I guess if my father had been Ambassador to Greenland I would still have retraced his footsteps." He paused and smiled down at her. "Maybe I'd be living in an igloo." He took her arm and guided her along the lawn. "I spent some of the happiest days of my life here," he said softly. "It was a time of innocence for me, before I . . ." He halted in midsentence, looked at her, and smiled. The mood had passed.

"Come on," he said. "I'll show you the river where Old Nick hangs out."

"Old who?"

But he had gone, jumping over the fence, running down the slope toward the river.

God above, Kate thought. Old Nick and the Son of Satan. Whatever next? And as she followed him, half stumbling, she realized that he had said nothing about Peter. It was unusual; nor had she thought about him all morning, and the realization made her feel guilty.

Damien stopped by the river's edge, standing on the bridge over a small brook which ran into the main stream, his hand on a wooden fence, looking down into a deep pool. Kate was panting slightly as she reached him, and she grabbed the fence for support.

"He's under there somewhere," Damien said, pointing. Kate peered into the depths, wondering what she was supposed to see. Horned monsters, cloven hooves, forked tails? What?

"Biggest pike you ever saw," Damien said.

"Oh, a fish," she said stupidly.

"He must be at least forty by now. We first met when I was four, and we've been on intimate terms ever since."

"You know, Old Nick is the name for the Devil over here," she said quickly, the words spilling out before she could think.

"Sure I know. And it's a great name for a pike."

She squinted at him, groping for a reaction. "Do you believe in God?" The question came out fast. But if Damien heard, he took no notice, merely smiled and bent lower.

"Look, there he goes."

"Where?" Kate leaned against the fence, following his pointed finger.

"There . . . look."

She heard the crack, felt herself topple, and had time to scream before she hit the water, her mouth open, legs and arms flailing, thinking in that instant that she was going to fall into the great jaws of the pike. Then she was under, the shock of the cold water sucking the breath from her. Eyes closed, she surfaced and sprayed water in the air like a whale. Fifty yards away, through blurred eyes, she could make out the weir by the house and the river rushing over it, swirling toward her. She went down again, feeling her feet touching the bottom, and the weeds grasping at her ankles. In a panic she kicked out and flapped her arms.

As she surfaced again, she saw Damien staring at her. He seemed to be smiling, but her vision was distorted by the water. Reaching out, she grabbed the broken stump of the fence post and clung to it. The current was strong, and it took all her strength to bring her free hand through the water and up onto the stump. But now she was safe, clinging there, half frozen, half drowned.

Damien dropped to his knees, leaned forward, and grabbed her wrist. She let go of the stump and allowed him to pull her out, his arms around her, dragging her to the bank, where she lay retching and spitting, deaf from the water in her ears. She stumbled to her feet and shook herself like a dog. Her ears clicked, and she heard him mutter in her ear that she needed some fresh clothes. Then his arms were around her, helping her up the slope, and she clung to him all the way back to the house.

She sat in front of the fire watching the logs burn, pulling a comb through her hair. Now that the shock had gone, she realized that she had never felt better. She reached for the glass and sipped the brandy. The shower had left her body tingling, and his bathrobe was rough on her skin, bringing up gooseflesh. She thought that she could feel the down on her legs wafting by the fire. Her eyes were bright and clear. Fall in the river, she said to herself, and feel like a million dollars.

In her mind she could see him again, just standing there smiling down at her as if to say—what? "Save *yourself?*" She did not know. She never knew what he was thinking. Everything about Damien Thorn was mysterious. All she knew was that he was the only man with the power to make her feel passive. She smiled. Her feminist friends would vomit at the idea, and she did not fancy it much herself.

But she had never been given to self-deception, and she luxuriated in the feeling that with Damien she could hand over responsibility for herself. Let him take control, let him make the running. She had never felt like this before, not as an adolescent, not even with Frank, and certainly not since Frank.

She heard him enter the room, but she did not turn.

"There should be something here to fit you," he said. Still she stared into the fire, feeling him move beside her.

"This looks about right." She turned, her cheeks pink from the heat of the flames. He was looking down at her, holding up a green shirt.

"Green or gray," he said, "depending on your mood."

She reached for the shirt, brushed it aside, and

touched his hand. The shirt fell to the floor, and when she spoke, the words came out as a whisper.

"Right now I feel like a moth that's flown too close to the flame."

He smiled at her and, with his index finger, traced a circle on her palm.

"But who is the moth?" he asked.

It had been so long, six months perhaps, and she had not realized how much she had missed it. In the first frenzy they had torn at one another, all the way out of the room, up the stairs and along the corridor to his bedroom. There was neither the need nor the desire for subtlety. For six months she had unwittingly stored up her fever, and now it was time. . . .

"Come with me." She tore at his hair as he reared above her. She reached for him, her arms around his shoulders, pulling him deeper, but he was resisting, his eyes closed, as if in pain.

"What is it?" She gripped his shoulders, but he pulled back, shaking his head.

"Please, Damien." She could not understand it. What could be wrong? It had been so good up until now. He could not stop, not now, for God's sake, he must not stop. . . .

"No good," he grunted. "Can't love. *Won't* love."

"Yes, Damien," she pleaded. "Love me." Desperately she tried to think what to do. Maybe he wanted her to be coarse, but she could never say the dirty words. They always stuck in her throat.

Now he was leaning over her, glaring at her, and in her imagination his eyes seemed to be tinged with yellow. "Do you want to see what I see?" he said.

She shook her head, trying to comprehend, knowing only one thing.

"I want *you*," she pleaded.

But he reared back, gone, out from inside her, ignoring her cries, and she felt herself being roughly turned onto her stomach, her face pressed into the pillow, his body heavy on her once more, and she tried to tell him, tried to say that she did not like it this way, that it was perverse, unnatural, but she could not get the words out, and he was too strong for her.

She raised her head from the pillow and grasped the rail of the bedstead, trying to force him away, but the more she struggled the quicker he moved.

His voice was hoarse in her ear. "Pain conquers all things," he whispered, his teeth on her neck. "Birth is pain. Death is pain. Beauty is pain."

"Love me, Damien." It was all she could say, even as she realized it no longer made any sense.

"I give you my pain, for love too is pain. . . ."

She placed her arms around her head, trying to shut out his words, twisting her face, but she could not escape his hands on her back, the nails clawing into her skin.

She turned and looked over her shoulder and saw his body stretched above her, his face turned to the ceiling as if in prayer.

"Show her true pain, Father!" he shouted. "Not the shallow thorns of earthly torment but the raptures of divinest anguish. . . ."

And she gave in to him, even as he roared, moving with him, helping him, crying out, the cry of a woman mingling with the triumphant howl of a beast.

It was dark when she awoke. Instinctively she reached across the bed for warmth, but she was alone. She sat up, slipped naked from the bed, and moved slowly to the door. In the mirror she could see the bruises and scratches on her back and neck. She shivered and crept into the corridor.

She whispered his name, but there was nothing, only the emptiness of the house. She tiptoed along the gallery, looked down into the hall, searching for him in the night.

It took her five minutes to find the chapel. She pushed the door open, and at first she did not see him in the gloom, only the white body of Christ nailed to the cross. She shook as she looked at it, grimacing in horror at the sight, then, as her eyes became accustomed to the dark, she saw him lying at the foot of the cross, naked and curled up in sleep, his knees drawn up to his chest, his arms wrapped around them.

"Damien?" Still a whisper, but he did not move.

She tiptoed forward, bent toward him, and touched his back. He was cold. She reached forward and stroked his hair, then glanced up again at the cross, at the tortured figure above her. When she looked down again, her fingers had drawn a parting in Damien's hair, and there, quite clearly now, she could see the three numbers that made up the mark of the beast.

666.

She closed her eyes and remained for a moment on her knees, then stood up and turned away. She did not look back as she left the room and no longer attempted to control the sobs as the tears ran unchecked down her face and between her breasts.

And in the darkness, Damien opened his eyes, two pinpricks of light, glowing yellow.

19

As if things were not bad enough already, Harvey Dean found a posse of reporters waiting for him at the elevator block inside the embassy when he arrived for work the next morning. He glared at the security men, and they shrugged back at him. How the press had gotten inside he did not know, but he did not have time to think about it.

There was no attempt at formality. They closed around him like scavengers.

"Was Schroeder on the Thorn payroll?" asked one.

"I'm sorry, gentlemen," said Dean, pushing through and hitting the elevator button. "No comment."

"Why can't we talk to Ambassador Thorn?" asked another.

"Because he's unavailable at the present time." Dean stared at the doors, willing them to open.

"Where is he?"

They had no manners, these people. None whatsoever. The door opened, and Dean gratefully stepped inside, the security men pushing the reporters back.

From the safety of the elevator Dean raised his hands and shrugged at them. "When the Ambassador's ready to make a statement, we'll let you know."

They howled at him, but the doors closed in their faces and he wiped his brow as he was whisked up through the shaft.

He moved fast, head down, toward the office, ignoring the secretaries. He opened the door and stood rigid as he saw Damien sitting behind the desk. He was the last person in the world Dean wanted to see.

"I thought you were up at the house," he said.

Damien said nothing.

"The reporters are going crazy for a statement on Schroeder," Dean continued. "I guess I can hold them off until you've talked to Buher, but you're going to have to—"

"What was De Carlo doing at your house yesterday?" Damien cut in. He delivered the words in a monotone, his face expressionless.

"Who?" And this time Dean was not acting dumb. Who the hell was De Carlo?

Damien was angry. He stood up, glaring at Dean. "Knock it off. Just give me the truth."

Dean shrugged. What was there to say?

Damien shook his head, looked at him in disgust, then turned and shouted, "Peter!"

A side door opened, and the boy was framed in the doorway. He stood for a moment as if in a dream, then moved forward, his feet dragging.

"Go ahead, Peter," Damien said softly.

The boy took out a notebook from his back pocket and opened it. When he spoke, he talked like a policeman at a court hearing.

"At half past three yesterday afternoon, I saw the priest called De Carlo go to number 114 Abbey Crescent, where he spent an hour and twenty-two minutes talking to the wife of Mr. Dean."

Dean lost control, the suppressed anxiety flooding out of him. Ignoring Peter, he turned beseechingly toward Damien. "Listen, I didn't know who he was," he said. "I mean—Barbara never told me she—"

"Destroy your son."

Dean shook his head and stepped back as if he had walked into a door. His mouth opened, but no words came out.

"There's only one boy left," said Damien. "And that's your son." The tone was matter-of-fact and calm. "Destroy him," he repeated. "Or be destroyed."

Dean shook his head and backed toward the door, panic rising in him. "No, no . . ." he stammered, still shaking his head, no longer conscious of what he was saying. "For God's sake, Damien . . ."

Damien ignored the blasphemy and stood firm, his arms folded. " 'And God said unto Abraham, "Take now thy son thine only Isaac whom thou lovest, and offer him for a burnt offering." ' "

Dean bumped into the wall and edged sideways toward the door, his fingers searching for the handles.

"If Abraham was ready to slay his own son for the love of his God," Damien continued, staring into his eyes, "why won't you do the same for the love of mine?"

Dean could not find the words. His tongue had frozen in his mouth. Only his legs seemed to work. He jerked at the double doors and fled, all dignity forgotten, stumbling past the secretaries and out toward the elevators.

Peter watched him go and looked up at Damien.

"Aren't you going to stop him?" he asked.

Damien shook his head. "There's no need," he said.

For the first time in their marriage, when they were both under the same roof, Barbara Dean had slept alone. She had dragged the couch into the baby's room and slept within arm's reach of the cot. Three times during the night she got up to make sure he was all right.

Over breakfast she and Harvey had said very little. She had already had her say, and if something was not done that evening, she was going to leave, with or without him.

Earlier that morning, she had put down the phone and nodded in satisfaction. The woman had agreed to put her up for a while. A friend of Carol's who had said twice, when they had met, that she must come and visit. They were so lonely down in Sussex. And so she had taken her up on the invitation. If the woman had been surprised at the suddenness of the request, she had done well to hide it. Barbara smiled wryly. Down in Sussex they would be wondering just what had happened. They would be gossiping happily—why is she leaving home? Have they had a fight? Will Harvey come or not?

The arrangements made, she had some ironing to do and then the packing. She set up the board and poured water into the steam iron. The baby lay in its portable cot under the window, the sun slanting onto his face. He gurgled and reached out at the sunlight as if to touch the beams, his hands making shadows on his face.

As she worked, Barbara looked over constantly at him. Twice she moved across to check that he was okay. The second time she saw that he had fallen asleep, his hands over his face. She moved his arms, tucked them under the cover, and went back to work. Soon she would be finished and before long she would be gone, she and her baby, and perhaps her husband.

The dog padded silently across the grass, moving purposefully. When it reached the edge of the Heath it stopped, sniffed the air, and set off along the avenue. No one came near it, neither dogs nor children. It made two turns and then stopped at a driveway. The hackles had risen now, and it bared its teeth in a snarl, then moved to the side of the house, nose twitching, following a scent. At the kitchen window it raised itself onto its hind legs, the front paws on the sill, and gazed down through the open window into the face of the baby. The dog's yellow eyes were unblinking; its saliva dripped onto the blanket.

When Barbara yelled, it looked up for a moment, gazed at her, then dropped to the ground and trotted slowly up the drive again, its work done.

Barbara slammed the window shut, shaking the glass. She leaned back against the frame, feeling her heart pound. The dog had given her such a shock, appearing like that. Muttering to herself, she glanced at the baby. He had turned in his sleep and was lying on his face, his feet twitching as if he were running in his dreams.

"It's okay, honey," Barbara said. "The nasty dog has gone."

She bent, turned the baby over, and then gazed in horror at her child. Staring back at her was an old wizened face, with rheumy eyes sunk in their sockets, the skin lined and brown. The baby reached for her with stained, arthritic, clawlike hands as she backed off, her mouth open in a scream, but no sound emerged, just a whimper, as she reached out for something, her hand finding only the handle of the iron. And the baby gazed back at her with dying eyes.

Harvey Dean drove five yards behind the motorcycle policeman, slicing through the traffic toward the Heath. In his rush to get home he had driven through a red light. The policeman who stopped him saw his CD plates, accepted his apology and his explanation, and decided to escort him home. By doing so, the policeman reckoned he might get some kind of commendation and at the same time ensure that no one got killed by a reckless Yank diplomat.

Dean turned into his driveway and rushed to the house, ignoring the policeman's goodbye wave. He threw open the door and stood in the hall. She would be glad, he thought. Now that the decision had been made, he felt better. At least now there was no battling with alternatives. He would run, with his family, and take his chances with the future.

"Barbara?"

The house was silent. No radio, no movement. He frowned and looked into the living room.

"Barbara?"

He pushed open the kitchen door and saw her standing by the ironing board, her back to him. He glanced across at the portable cot and saw the baby's arm, the perfect little fingers raised stiffly in the air as if in salute.

"What's the matter, Barbara, didn't you hear me?"

Still she did not turn. He moved forward, frowning. "I want you to start packing. We're getting out—"

She turned, and he stopped, aghast. Her eyes were

red with tears, her face twisted into a snarl. He stepped back as she sprang at him, and the last thing he saw was her arm swinging toward him and the pointed end of the steam iron as she plunged it into his eye.

His agonized scream combined with the hiss of the iron as the heated metal evaporated his eye in a belch of steam. His body slithered to the floor, the shattered eyesocket weeping matter from the nether regions of his brain in a tearlike trickle down his blistered cheek.

Barbara carefully placed the iron on the board, then bent to touch his shoulder. Peering at him, she could see through his smashed eye into the very center of his brain. She got up, moved to the sink, picked up a cloth, bent again to her husband, and gently wiped away the gray slime which ran down his face. When she had finished she went back to her baby, touched the pink fingers, and gazed into his battered face.

Then she sat down at the table, smiled to herself, and went completely and incurably mad.

20

In the past week Father De Carlo had passed well beyond the normal limits of human endurance. He had eaten little and had hardly slept, sustained by his faith and by his God, bolstered by the indescribable joy of seeing the Christ Child and the privilege of acting as His protector. His body wanted to rest, but his mind would not permit it. He was forcing himself to continue until the task was over, and only then would he give in.

In the taxi taking him through the West End, he gazed at the people going about their business. How he envied them their trivial everyday problems. One man reminded him of Antonio, and again, for the hundredth time, he bent his head, praying for the souls of the six men. When he looked up, his face was streaked with tears, and he brushed them away with his sleeve. Sometimes the sorrow and despair threatened to overcome him, and he only hoped that his life would be spared until the Anti-Christ was dead and the Holy Child was safe and secure to rule over His Kingdom.

He checked his notebook. In the past few days he had surprised himself by his cunning. Alone, he had supervised the hiding of the Baby. Alone, he had kept track of Thorn's movements and those of the woman and her son. He permitted himself a small measure of pride. He would have made a very good detective.

"BBC, guv," the taxi driver shouted over his shoulder.

Father De Carlo thanked him and clambered from the cab. The building was in darkness, and he knew from experience that Kate Reynolds did not leave until the last minute. There was no one at the door, and he gave thanks for a small degree of luck. At least he would not have to wait in the cold. He could go right on in and catch her before she left.

The studio was almost deserted. Kate slipped the last of her notes into a file and placed them by her chair. She looked up and smiled as two technicians shouted goodnight at her, then got up from her desk, stretched, and moved into the shadows, looking for her coat.

A voice echoed through the studio. "Locking up in five minutes, Miss Reynolds."

"Coming," she shouted back. Normally she was glad to be gone, another program successfully over, but tonight she had dreaded this moment.

"Miss Reynolds." The voice behind her startled her. She turned and glared angrily at the priest. How had the man gotten in? He was always turning up in the dark, scaring her.

"What are you doing here?"

"You saw him, didn't you, Miss Reynolds?"

He looked ill. Even in the darkness she was aware of the hollowness in his cheeks, the tired eyes, and the droop of his shoulders.

"You know now that Thorn is the Anti-Christ," he continued. Moving forward, he touched her arm. "So why are you protecting him?"

Kate snatched her arm away from him. "Either you get out of here or I'll call security." She looked over her shoulder, searching through the shadows, the anger boiling inside her. If security wasn't around, she would personally throw the priest out, and head-first if necessary.

"Your son, Miss Reynolds. Where is he?"

"In bed and asleep, of course," she said irritably.

Father De Carlo shook his head. "No, he is not. Your son is with Damien Thorn."

Kate turned and stared at him.

"*With* him, Miss Reynolds," he continued, emphasizing the first word. "With him in body and soul. Your son has become an apostle of the Anti-Christ."

Kate let out a sound of mirthless laughter. She was sick to death of all this. All she wanted was for this man to get out of her sight.

"You think Peter has been in school for the past three days, don't you?"

Kate nodded, humoring him.

"Check with them if you don't believe me. Make a phone call." Father De Carlo saw the change in her expression, the doubt and fear replacing anger. "Peter has been working for Thorn," he continued. "He is a disciple in evil, conspiring to murder the Christ Child, but they won't succeed. The Holy Child is beyond his powers now. He is safe, but your child is not."

She shook her head and frowned.

"There is only one way to save Peter, Miss Reynolds, and that is by destroying the Anti-Christ." He reached into his jacket and drew out the dagger. Kate looked at it, her eyes wide in horror.

"You're asking me to . . ." She stopped, unable to go on, staring at the blade.

"No, Miss Reynolds. That is to be my sacred task. But if you value your son's immortal soul, you must help me to carry it out."

She stood looking again into the shadows and back at the dagger. Father De Carlo gazed at her, concentrating, willing her to help him. If she did not help, then there was little hope left.

"Hurry along, Miss Reynolds," the voice of the guard echoed again. "Locking up!"

The man's voice seemed to bring Kate back to reality.

"Coming," she shouted, and when she turned back to Father De Carlo, she was in control of herself once more.

"I'm going home to my son," she said.

"Then I beg you to let me come with you," said Father De Carlo. "There will be no time to lose when you find he is not there."

Kate shrugged and moved away. She could not keep him from following her. She would show Peter to him, take him up and point the boy out, then perhaps the man would go away and leave her alone.

"Peter!"

There were no lights in the flat. Surely he was not asleep already. Since his last birthday, he frequently stayed up late, reading or playing records. But the flat was silent and in darkness.

Father De Carlo waited in the living room while

Kate went to the boy's bedroom. When she returned he saw her expression and felt pity for her.

"You were right," she said flatly.

He picked up the telephone and handed it to her. She dialed and waited.

"Mrs. Grant? Sorry to call so late. It's Kate Reynolds . . ."

He gazed into the street as she finished her call.

"Right again," she said, putting down the receiver. A thought crossed her mind. "Are you saying that he was at Pereford last night?"

"I'm afraid so."

"Oh my God." She sat down, close to tears, hands clasped so that her knuckles showed white.

He sat next to her, and this time she did not move away. "Will you help?" he asked.

"Of course."

The route was familiar to her now. She had no need to check maps or road signs, and as she drove, she tried to concentrate on Father De Carlo's words.

"I know you have read about the Thorn tragedies," he was saying. "But you know only half of it."

She glanced curiously at him.

"A priest," he said quietly. "Father Tassone, a tragic man who had helped at the birth. Later he tried to repent, tried to warn Robert Thorn." He paused. "Dead," he added simply.

He raised his right hand and began to make points on his fingers. "A photographer called Jennings who tried to help Robert Thorn. Decapitated."

Kate shivered and clutched the wheel until her knuckles showed white.

"Six years later," he continued. "Bugenhagen, the archaeologist. Buried underground." He was talking faster now and running out of fingers. "Bill Atherton . . ."

"Yes," said Kate. "I read about him."

"Joan Hart," he said in the same tone. "A journalist like yourself. Dead. Dr. Charles Warren, curator of the Thorn Museum, found impaled by the—"

"Stop," said Kate, her face white, her voice trembling. "I don't want to hear."

"Very well," said Father De Carlo. "I shall tell you a wonderful story." He closed his eyes. "We saw the alignment, you know—the three suns. Up until then it was the most wonderful experience of my life. After two thousand years, the Second Coming."

Kate relaxed a little, driving the images of dead men and women from her mind.

"Then we went looking for Him. It was simple. The astronomer gave us the exact location of His birth, and we found Him." He stopped, savoring the moment. "Among gypsies."

Kate snapped her head around and stared at the priest.

"He is the most beautiful, the most gracious creature." He smiled and turned toward her. "That is the irony, you see. There is no birth certificate. The gypsies have no need of them. So all these children were murdered. And for what?"

"And your friend, the monk," she said. "He died for nothing."

"Not only him," said Father De Carlo softly.

"There were others?"

"Oh yes."

Kate lifted one hand from the wheel. "Well, don't tell me," she said. "I can't take any more."

"No, I understand. But there is one thing more." And despite her protests he told her about the birth of

186

Damien; the stone killing the baby, the dreadful birth which split the womb of the jackal.

"A what?" she said, turning to look at him, almost losing control of the car. Through her clothes she could feel the scratches and bites, and she shivered, recalling the animal-like thrusting, the words he had used, the sounds he had made. It was an abomination. She wanted to scrub herself till she bled, and she knew that never again would she feel clean.

"Here," said Father De Carlo. "We are here. I will leave you here now to do what must be done."

She stopped and watched him leave, then turned the car and set off again, toward Peter. When it was over she would take him away, go on holiday, hold him in her arms for a month and never let him out of her sight, until the scars were healed on both of them.

At the gate, the security guard smiled at her and said that the Ambassador was expecting her. She was not surprised. She was no longer capable of being surprised at anything.

The chapel was in darkness, but Peter could see what he needed to see. He gazed at the cross and at Damien standing before it.

"So you think you have won, do you?" Damien said to the back of Christ's head. "You have watched me slay a hundred children in your place, and you have never lifted a finger to save them."

He sneered and moved around to stare into the agonized face pressed against the wood of the cross.

"But that has been your game all along, hasn't it? Playing hide and seek across the ages. Well, now it's over."

He glanced back at Peter, then back at the cross.

"Suffer the little children to come unto me," he said sarcastically. "Your words, Nazarene. Not mine."

He took hold of Peter's hand and raised his eyes to the ceiling. "O Satan, beloved Father, the victory is thine. All praise to thee, for thou hast delivered this virgin child unto me that I may face the Nazarene at last."

He turned again and dropped to his knees, staring into Peter's face and holding both his hands.

"I want you to listen to me, Peter," he said. "And listen carefully. Your mother is on her way up here to take you away from me."

Peter shook his head and tried to draw away. "No, Damien, don't send me back to her."

Damien smiled. "Don't worry. From this moment on, you belong to me."

He touched the boy's face, his hands cupping Peter's chin.

"The Christian faith has ten commandments," he said softly. "I have only one."

Peter nodded. In the corridor Damien heard footsteps, but he did not turn. He continued gazing into Peter's face.

"Say it now and we two shall become as one."

"I love you," said Peter.

"Beyond all others," Damien coaxed.

"Beyond all others."

"Beyond life itself."

"Beyond life itself."

Damien sighed and bowed his head as Kate pushed the door open behind him.

"I am here to make the deal, Damien," she said.

Peter twitched, startled. He tried to turn, but Damien held him fast.

"Where is he?" Damien asked, still looking into Peter's eyes.

"Give me back my son and I will lead you to him," said Kate.

Peter shook his head and twisted in Damien's grip. "No, Damien, I'm not her son. I belong to you."

Damien heard the groan escape from Kate's lips, and he smiled, then turned and looked at her for the first time, seeing her in the doorway, standing erect, too erect, as if she were trying to stop shaking.

"Lead us to the Nazarene," he said. "Then you can have Peter back."

The boy wriggled in his grasp and shook his head. "No, Damien, it's a trick."

"Not if she wants her son back, it isn't," said Damien, looking from one to the other.

Kate nodded in agreement and slumped against the door, staring into Peter's eyes as he walked past her, still clutching Damien's hand.

She shook her head and closed her eyes as if to shut out the sight of him. Peter, her only child, had become a hostile, sneering stranger. She could not accept it, *would* not accept it.

"Let's go," said Damien.

She looked up at the cross. Everything had gone to pieces. It was not meant to happen this way. And now she had no choice but to lead her son into a trap. He was the one human being she would give her life to protect, and now she was helplessly exposing him to danger.

"If you can help me," she whispered to the tortured Christ, "then help me now."

21

Even now she could not take it in. The enormity of the situation escaped her. She had never believed, not since childhood; she had no faith, either in a god or in a devil. It was impossible. Soon she would awake from this awful nightmare. Peter would be standing by her bed with her glass of fruit juice and some boyish sarcastic comment.

She glanced in the driving mirror, and two pairs of eyes looked back at her, each eye tinged with yellow. She shuddered, and her hands slipped on the wheel. They were talking together behind her, whispering like conspirators, and she was consumed with a jealous rage. Suddenly she thought of her husband, Frank. Tears welled and began to cloud her vision. She wiped them away. Thank God he had never known about this. As he was dying he had pleaded with her to give the boy a father, and she had promised him. And now this. . . .

She tried to think, but her reasoning no longer functioned. Ideas raced through her mind, spilling one upon the other. She could crash the car perhaps, drive it into the ditch, take a chance on Peter being hurt; but no. If she hurt him she would never be able to forgive herself. She could stop a policeman; but no policeman would ever believe her. She could drive until the car ran out of gasoline, and when Damien was looking at the engine, she could—

"Are we nearly there?" Peter's voice broke in.

"Two miles," said Damien.

She blinked and tried not to cry. He knew. He could read her mind. He had access to her innermost thoughts. Behind her, he must be smirking at her puny attempts to outwit him. She gave up and concentrated on the road. It was narrow, flanked with high hedges. Small furry creatures scurried into the bushes. A hare loped ahead of her, made a swift decision, and darted away to its left to safety. Insects splattered themselves against the windscreen, but there was no one around, no other cars, no one walking. It was a bright night and the stars blinked down at her, but there was no cloud, no movement. It was as if the world were holding its breath.

She reached the crest of a hill and saw the silhouette of a vast ruined cathedral, its towers rearing a hundred feet into the night sky. Peter gasped. In the mirror she could see him cover his eyes and turn his head as if the sight were painful, but Damien stared forward, licking his lips in anticipation.

She shifted gears, sending a screech through the car, causing a flock of crows to lift, cawing from the trees. She heard Damien curse at her, and in the mirror she saw him put his arm around Peter, holding him close as if to protect him.

191

A terrible hatred grew within her as she watched him. It was his destiny. She remembered him looking at his house, talking wistfully about his childhood and his lost innocence. Well, to Hell with his destiny and his innocence and to Hell with him; his soul could go back to Hell where it belonged.

There was only one consolation—that at least his abominable seed had not lodged in her womb. She could not have borne that.

Fifty yards from the cathedral, she stamped on the brake and switched off the ignition. In the sudden stillness she forced her brain to function.

"Let me go on ahead," she said. Just you and me, Damien, she pleaded silently. Just you and me. Leave Peter in the car. Please!

"We all go together," Damien said.

She turned and stared at him. Surely he would permit her this one thing. "Trust me, Damien," she said. "I just want to make sure—"

"No." It was Peter who was shaking his head. "Don't trust her."

Peter turned and clambered out of the car, Damien behind him. They stood waiting for Kate, man and boy, hand in hand. Kate looked at them for a moment, then swung herself out of the driving seat. I have no choice, she thought. It was out of her hands now.

"You lead the way," Damien said.

She looked up at the cathedral. It was bleak and empty, a crumbling monument to a neglected God. By the massive doorway, masonry and pillars lay where they had fallen. Anxiously she searched the darkness but could see no one in the shadows.

"Go on," Peter commanded her, his voice impatient.

She moved slowly forward, her legs trembling, so that she was afraid she might fall. The Christ Child born among gypsies; and still she did not believe. She did not even care; all that mattered was the dagger. . . .

Ten yards from the doorway she stopped, sensing Damien a pace behind her. She could almost smell his anticipation.

"In there," she said, pointing to the hatch set into the doorway.

"Open it," Damien whispered.

She stepped forward and reached for the handle and in the corner of her eye she saw Father De Carlo move from behind a pillar, the dagger in his hand, and she shouted instinctively.

"No, Father!"

Father De Carlo hesitated just long enough for Damien to turn, pulling Peter with him, and as the priest leaped, Damien twisted the boy around and lifted him high in the air. Father De Carlo could not stop. The force of his momentum took him forward. The dagger, already driven toward Damien, caught Peter squarely in the back.

"*Peter!*" Kate screamed as Damien hurled the boy to the ground and leaped for the priest, his hand reaching for the older man's throat, forcing him back against the stone wall.

"Peter!" She rushed forward, stumbling, falling to her knees, as the boy crawled on all fours like an animal, the dagger protruding from his back.

"Oh, my darling . . ." Why had she shouted? Why had she warned him? She held Peter's face and stared into his eyes. "Don't leave me, Peter. . . ."

But his eyes were already cloudy, and his breath rasped in his throat.

"Don't die, please don't die. . . ."

"I love you," he murmured.

"Peter . . ."

"Beyond life itself. I love you, Damien. . . ." He smiled, closed his eyes, and slumped into her arms.

"No, Peter, no . . ."

For a moment she stared at him, then gently turned him over, drew breath, pulled the dagger with two hands from his back, laid him on the grass, and looked up.

Damien had forced Father De Carlo to his knees. He was bending over him, throttling the priest, and he did not see Kate move quickly toward him. Her scream of rage shattered the silence as she thrust the dagger forcefully into his spine. It grated against bone, and she pushed even further, twisting viciously until it was embedded to the hilt. Then she stepped back as her screams echoed wildly among the dark ruins.

Damien stood erect, his hands reaching for the dagger. He grunted, dropped to his knees, dragged himself to his feet again, and stumbled against the doorway, forcing it open.

For a moment he stood motionless, the yellow eyes searching the vast emptiness, gazing up at the walls towering a hundred feet all around him.

"Nazarene," he roared. "Where are you, Nazarene?"

He swayed and stumbled, fighting to keep upright.

"Do you hear me, Nazarene?"

As if in reply, a light flickered dimly at the far end of the building, a hazy halo, steadily growing brighter. Damien grunted and moved toward it, his legs moving swiftly, quickening to a run, a weaving sprint, his arms outstretched, moving fast, like a man who has been tripped at speed and staggers out of control. His back was arched, his face twisted in pain, eyes staring through the shattered roof above him.

"Satan," he roared. "Why has thou deserted me?"

The sound of his voice came back to him, and the light before him grew in intensity.

He fell to his knees and groveled on all fours.

"It's over, Father," he whispered. "Receive me back into thy paradise."

His body trembled, then he pitched slowly forward onto his face and lay still.

The light was blinding now, but Father De Carlo gazed into it unblinking. He looked down at Kate kneeling by the body of her son, touched her hair, and made the sign of the cross over the boy's eyes. Kate rose, as Father De Carlo lifted Peter in his arms, and together they stood, the woman and the priest, gazing into the light, their tears bright upon their cheeks.

It was dawn. The conflict had been resolved. A new era had begun.

And God shall wipe away all tears from their eyes; and there shall be no more death, neither sorrow, nor crying; neither shall there be any more pain: for the former things are passed away.

And he that sat upon the throne said, Behold I make all things new. . . .

Behold I come quickly: blessed is he that keepeth the sayings of the prophecy of this book.

—REVELATIONS 21: 4, 5; 22: 7

ABOUT THE AUTHOR

GORDON McGILL was born in Glasgow in 1943, and worked on local newspapers before going to Fleet Street in 1968. He wrote his first novel, ARTHUR, in 1972, and spent two years working as a freelance journalist in New York. Since returning to London, he has been writing full-time. His suspense novel, WAR STORY, was recently published in America to critical acclaim.

Big Bestsellers from SIGNET

Great Reading from SIGNET

- [ ] **THE DARK** by James Herbert. (#E9403—$2.95)
- [ ] **THE SPEAR** by James Herbert. (#E9060—$2.50)*
- [ ] **LAIR** by James Herbert. (#E8650—$2.25)
- [ ] **FLUKE** by James Herbert. (#J8394—$1.95)
- [ ] **THE RATS** by James Herbert. (#E8770—$1.75)
- [ ] **THE FOG** by James Herbert. (#J9193—$1.95)
- [ ] **THE SURVIVOR** by James Herbert. (#E9707—$2.25)
- [ ] **KILLER** by Peter Tonkin. (#E9241—$2.50)
- [ ] **THE SPIDERS** by Richard Lewis. (#E9250—$1.75)*
- [ ] **THE BLACK HORDE** by Richard Lewis. (#E9454—$1.75)
- [ ] **THE SUMMER VISITORS** by Brooke Leimas.
  (#J9247—$1.95)*
- [ ] **THE INTRUDER** by Brooke Leimas. (#E9524—$2.50)*
- [ ] **KILLER CRABS** by Guy N. Smith. (#E8954—$1.75)
- [ ] **THE ANTS** by Peter Tremayne. (#E9163—$1.75)†

* Price slightly higher in Canada
† Not available in Canada

Recommended SIGNET Books

Buy them at your local
bookstore or use coupon
on next page for ordering.

𝒪

Great Reading from SIGNET